CLOSE TO THE SILENCE

Dancing while we may, 4

Kevin Corby Bowyer

Mysterious Strawberry

CONTENTS

exactly the same length.

Three years after its first release, this book still makes me smile and laugh. That is good.

The original *Author's Preface*, dated February 8, 2021, has been removed from this revision. It strikes me now as too flippant, too self-conscious. It can still be found on my website, should anyone wish to read it.

Kevin Corby Bowyer, Muirkirk, January 10, 2024

* As for Leafy Crosthwaite, her story is now fully expounded in *Babylon House* and *Cadmun Gale.*

1.

Ethel – the house
otherwise, mostly milkmaids

She's sitting on the bench near the apple tree, waiting for me to do something.

"The whole book," she said. "I waited and waited… and what kind of a mention did I get?" She shook her head, *typical*, and I felt a bit guilty.

But she's not the only one; others are waiting. I guess some of them don't know yet that they have their own stories to tell. Maybe some don't care. Perhaps some are not even self-aware.

But I doubt that.

Ethel is impatient – angry. I gave her just enough of a twist to wake her up and make her want to get on with it. She hates men. She hates me. She sits there by the apple tree, glum, forty-three years old, dressed in her nun's habit. Not that she actually *is* a nun – it's just an aspiration, and a way of expressing her loathing for men.

You always let me down, she thinks. *Men. Three times I entrusted my love to them – three times – and always had it kicked back. Well, now you can bugger off – the lot of you. It's too late.*

I watch her through my kitchen window. She's twisting something in her hands, waiting. But she won't move from there till I say. And that'll be some time yet.

Miserable and grey. Ethel Coombs.

The house. It stands alone – no other dwellings nearby. It's built of a very dark stone, like it absorbs the daylight. I stand in the grounds (I won't call them a garden yet, but I might later) and look at it, the house. I'm not sure how old it is. Could be nineteenth century but I think it's older than that – at least eighteenth. Fifteenth, maybe. Or older – much older. It depends. The house is stark and thin. The walls bow inwards, giving the appearance that it's starved, lost weight. The roof is slated and rises sharply, enclosing a tall attic space. I count six stories, but I know there are many more. I've never got to the top, although I've lived here for sixty years.

I look around me. The sun shines, but it's windy. The land is flat, or with just a few gentle rises too modest to be called hills. There are a few trees – a bit of woodland away somewhere, to the right – or the left; a road, way off at the front of the house, running past the gate. There's no-one in sight; no cars; no sign of people, although Tommy Widdop does occasionally drive along that road with mail for me. I think the sea is not far away. I'm not sure I could pinpoint the house on a map, but I think it may be in Yorkshire – North Yorkshire, probably. But maybe Scotland – it depends on the day.

The inside of the house is a bit like a lighthouse – or some kind of tower anyway. The rooms are arranged around a maze of central staircases, all constructed from dark oak. I stand in the middle, switch on the lights, and look up. My eyes follow the stairs as they rise – not circular, not square, but extending upwards in fits and starts, often at an uncomfortable angle. I can't see the top – it's too far away. But I dream about it sometimes – reaching the summit and stepping out onto the roof. I have an idea there may be a big pipe organ in the attic, but I don't think I'll ever see it. I used to hope I'd give it breath one day, but I've lost interest now.

There's a nude woman up there. I often hear her padding about and catch glimpses of soft pink. I don't know who it is. Not Kate, I think; Kate's way too busy to go stomping about my house. Might be Fuzzy. Certainly not Clara. The steps are too lively to be Janet, although it would be nice to see her. I wonder if it's Louise – Louise Flesher: intriguing, intellectual, withdrawn. Perhaps I haven't given her enough thought. She's probably lonely. But I think she'd be too dignified to run about, particularly without her clothes.

And the milkmaids are not here yet.

The sunset was memorable. I do get some amazing colours. Last night was dramatic – a soft glowing cerise at first, deepening to vermillion; then shocking red, like her hair. It was as if the sky was her hair. The impression was so strong that I thought I'd see her face looking down from behind the clouds, smiling in the pillows of the firmament.

But the sun continued to pack itself away, and the sky became full of blood, then the heavy dark of a fine wine. Finally, black. No stars – too overcast.

I didn't sleep well.

I heard the woman all night, hurrying around, sometimes just two or three floors up, sometimes further away, high in the spaces I could never get to. In my mind, I saw her feet on the wooden floors: her ankles, heels, insteps, toes, nails; the lines in the skin of her soles like the gentle valleys of an undiscovered land.

I got up a couple of times and sat by the window, but it was too dark to see if Ethel was still sitting by the apple tree. I hope she doesn't stay there all night; the front door is not locked. I imagine she has a room somewhere in the house, although I'm never aware of her presence inside, and she's always there by the apple tree when I look in the morning, dressed in her habit. I wonder if she sleeps in it; I can't imagine her in a nightgown.

I set her spinning and then left her. She resents that and wants to get on with her life, whatever it may be. She knows I didn't set her vibrating for nothing. Something's coming for her.

Is she frightened? It's possible.

They arrived this morning – the milkmaids and a couple of hangers-on. Delia Tweddle pushed open the door, called her soft "*cooee*," and I came running from the kitchen to greet her. She was smiley. Always kind, Delia. I got a kiss on the cheek and cuddled her. It was nice and squeezy, warm. I hung on, my arms about her, reluctant to let go – felt myself sighing. She didn't seem to mind. She has lovely, liquid eyes.

"Sukey and Theo aren't coming in," she said. "They want to go for a walk."

I looked past her and saw them ambling together, right to left across the path, tracing an anticlockwise track around the house. I'm disappointed but not surprised. They're already following their own threads, Theo with his mind on Clara, Sukey trying to keep him.

I heard Birdie Wade before I saw her. She was over by Ethel's bench, doubled up, coughing up her lungs. It should surprise me that she's still alive (although it doesn't, of course). Smokers' cough – no change all these years. Is she any closer to death? Probably. Who knows? Ethel was there in her usual place, watching Birdie splutter. She didn't move or offer help.

"We brought Birdie," said Delia, pulling away from me. "Hope you don't mind."

Of course I didn't mind. I'm responsible for all of them. Or are they responsible for me…?

Birdie doesn't come into the house but sits next to Ethel and lights her pipe. Neither offers a greeting to the other; perhaps they're communicating on a deeper level, like ants, or whales.

The others make themselves comfortable in my drawing room: smiley Delia, shy petite Fanny

Kirkbride, oddly enigmatic Leafy Crosthwaite, kindly Neva Hutton with her salt-and-pepper hair, and wiry little Flossie Ousby. Flossie arrived in the company of her husband, Zachariah (Rye). Rye is a big, strapping fellow, very different from his little wife, although they're both sparking with energy. He's physically impressive – just over six feet, I reckon. I don't want him in here – I only want the girls. So I send him off and away, up into the house, to look for the nude woman.

The five women are all dressed for a day out. They've left their milkmaiding gear at home. They wear nice bonnets, modest frocks (but nevertheless pretty, as suits the occasion) and charming smiles. I'm far too much of a gent to ask their ages, but I reckon my cuddly Delia to be twenty-seven. Leafy Crosthwaite is the oldest, I'd say – about thirty-five, possibly younger, but she's always struck me as a little worn-looking, a little lined. I bet there's a story there. The other three: sweet Fanny Kirkbride can't be older than twenty-two; Genevieve (Neva) Hutton is about thirty, and Florence (Flossie) Ousby about the same. Neva is the thoughtful one – always ready to listen, always keen to find a compromise.

I bring them tea and some biscuits and cakes I made yesterday. The five women sit across from me, demure, smiling prettily. I wonder if they're thinking the same as I am. Bet they're not.

I hear boots running high above, a thud, and a scream.

I point at Delia and raise my eyebrows, inviting

her to surrender her story.

"Well," she says, glancing at Neva, "Neva and me are both from Thorpe Bassett."

She looks at me, and I shrug *Where the hell's that?*

She enlightens me. "It's between York and Scarborough, a bit more than forty miles from the Lookout."

I raise a finger and wink at her; it was a good enough description. She's pleased, makes a funny little delighted noise, and wrinkles her nose. I like that and wrinkle mine back.

"Neva worked on a farm with her mum and dad and brothers, and I worked in the Royal Oak."

I enquire what drew them to the Lookout.

"It was meant to be an adventure," says Delia. "We came a few years after the school opened. 1759 I think it was…"

"'58," Neva corrects.

"1758," Delia repeats. "I wasn't even twenty. We thought it might be a bit of a lark, working in such a place…"

"Although we did like working at home too," says Neva. "It wasn't like we'd fallen out with anyone…"

The two women look at each and Delia interjects, "…or our mums and dads…"

"…or our brothers…," adds Neva.

"…or anyone," Delia finishes, rather lamely.

I assure them that I accept what they say but make a mental note they're hiding something and plan to mine the truth out of them later.

"We only meant to live at the school for a year or

so," says Delia.

"But we stayed," Neva concludes. There's a moment of silence; then she adds, "It was lovely."

The other women nod their heads as if in response to a prayer. I look out of the window and notice Theo and Sukey still walking widdershins round the house, probably on their second or third circuit.

There's a lot of noise far away upstairs – shouts, things being thrown. It sounds like the nude woman has been cornered.

I return my attention to the five milkmaids. They all watch me from beneath furrowed brows, their mouths open like stone figures in a fountain, about to gush claret. I focus on Leafy Crosthwaite and ask for her story.

She shakes her head and lowers her gaze. "I've been at the Lookout since it opened, sir," she says (I rather like this "sir"…). "I was taken in because of Mr Crowan's kindness. I can tell you no more – not yet anyway."

I like her – quite a lot, I realise – and decide not to press. I assure her I understand. She smiles at me. It's a nice smile – thoughtful, intriguing, intelligent…

Silence returns. My daydream dissolves.

I look at Fanny Kirkbride, open my mouth, and am teetering on the precipice of speech when Delia fires a brief statement into the room:

"We don't mind."

I'm puzzled and ask what she means.

She casts a rapid glance at the other women and

goes on: "We've all had a chinwag, and we all agree. We don't mind that you haven't spun our stories yet. We've been waiting – most of us – but we understand. We can't *all* be in the foreground."

I spread my fingers in... what? Apology? Helplessness? I'm not sure.

Delia turns out to be a bit of a chatterbox: "I mean, when you think about it, a book – a story – is really a *path*, isn't it? It selects from things that are happening and ignores the rest. I mean, if two people are talking in a field, the story tells us their words – and maybe a bit of what the weather's like, or what the birds are doing, or if cows are mooing nearby, or the voices of sheep, dogs, cats, maybe even other people – but it can't tell *everything* that happens at that moment in that place. I mean, maybe someone's dying in a cottage close by; p'raps there's a mole burrowing away beneath where the two people are standing... Or maybe the scene could be described from another point of view – what it looks like to a bird flying overhead – a hawk, maybe, or a gull. See what I mean? A story just takes selected bits of what's going on and steps through the event like stones across a river. You pick your path and ignore the rest."

I look at her, my eyes wide, eager to hear where she's going next.

"I mean," she says (it's her favourite introductory phrase), "suppose you rewrite that whole passage but ignore all the things you've already written about and just focus on the things you missed first time round? Then you'd have a kind of inverse story that would fit like a glove with the other one, even though the two narratives had nothing in common except the flow of time."

Bugger me! I think, in awe of her exposition, delivered with the overwhelming determination and thrust of an invading army. I'd hoped one day to be a writer, but I can't match such an intellect. I make a mental note to hang myself at some convenient moment – but then begin to think of my own death in terms of Delia's negative narrative. The centre of attention would no longer be in the rope, or in my neck, or in my failed life, but in the woodworm working away in the leg of the chair I kick away from beneath my feet.

But she's not done! She goes on, speaking rapidly and with total conviction: "I mean," (there it is again...), "*so far...*" (she emphasises the phrase, implying that the *so-faredness* would not be permitted to go on interminably), "...*we've* been in the inverse narrative – the girls and me..." (Delia gestures at them, and they all nod). "But it won't always be like that – I know."

(Hmmmm...)

She goes on. "When you think about all the things that don't get into literature... I mean, did Jesus never trip up? I mean, apart from when he was carrying the cross to Golgotha. Remember when he was teaching the people from Peter's boat? I mean, he in the boat, teaching – they onshore, listening? I mean, maybe he fell, getting out. *Behold, Jesus hopped out of the boat, intending to join the five thousand, but got his robe caught in the oar and went flying arse-over-tit* (begging your pardon) *into the Lake of Galilee. Splash!* I mean, it could have happened. It's not likely he got through his whole life without ever having an accident, is it?"

"Delia!" Neva exclaims. "That's blasphemous!"

But Delia isn't having it – and I allow her virtuoso monologue to flood on, breaking through the dam of her colleague's objection and inundating the plains of accepted wisdom:

"No, it's not!" she insists. "God came down from Heaven and became man to redeem us. If he was properly man, things must have gone wrong now and then – otherwise it wouldn't count. I mean, think of him turning all that water into wine at the wedding in Cana. He didn't make a big song and dance about it, did he? No, he didn't! But how many times had he practised that? I bet he couldn't have just done it straight off – he must've practised for hours and hours to get that right, but the rehearsals are not reported. See what I mean?"

She doesn't give me time to submit to her reasoning but builds her argument into two precipitous walls of water: "Or all the Egyptians drowned in the Red Sea. I mean, there were *hundreds of them!* All dead! They must have had families – wives and children who grieved for them, mums and dads who loved them and cared about them. But you never hear about them, do you? Because the story's not about *them* people; it's about the poor sods who got massacred. I'm right, aren't I?" She pauses, looks at me for endorsement, and adds apologetically, "I mean, not that I read or anything…" Her stare intensifies, eyes widening, lips pressing ever more firmly, demanding an answer.

Her analysis seems flawless, so I concur wholeheartedly.

She smiles, pleased, having got the thing so eloquently off her chest. And I reflect her happiness with a broad grin. She nods, and says confidently, "So, *our stories are coming.*"

I return her nod and assure her, yes, of course they are. She smiles again – and wrinkles her nose. It's pretty. I wrinkle back.

Out of the Noise of Space.

I signal to Flossie. She wasn't expecting it and jumps a bit, her shoulders bouncing.

"Me and Rye?" she says. "We don't have much of a story to tell."

I arrange my features to express mild incredulity. It's intended to prise detail from her. *Oh, come on,* it says. *Don't be modest.* (I practise these expressions for hours every week, sitting in front of my mirror. *Mild incredulity* is one of the easiest. Many are a good deal harder: *fearful encouragement* is one such; also, *disbelieving sympathy, terrified hilarity, perspicacious morbidity, penumbral joy* – the list is endless.)

Flossie opens her mouth to continue, but our discourse is briefly bayoneted by a bloodcurdling scream from above. It's her husband – it sounds like he's had something cut off. A woman cackles loudly and throws out a lengthy string of obscene invective. Neva grimaces and covers her ears. Delia, Fanny and Leafy continue to watch me, their waxen smiles undisturbed. Flossie is paused, expressionless, mouth open, ready to speak as soon as the interruption terminates.

Something comes whistling through the air in the stairwell just beyond the door and smashes to smithereens on the hall floor. None of us sees what it was, but I believe it must have been a chamber pot thrown from one of the upstairs bedrooms. I don't think I've emptied them in the last month, so I steel myself to a session with the mop later in the day. I wonder if I might get the ladies to clear it up…

Nothing further occurs, and we allow the silence to settle, half-expecting some form of commotion or attack to ensue – but it doesn't. There are no more voices, no more projectiles. Five seconds… ten… fifteen… Delia, Fanny, Leafy and Neva exchange glances. One of my clocks strikes four; another, ten.

Flossie's countenance reanimates, and she reveals her story:

"Rye and me used to work on the docks at Whitby. Rye (you can see how strong he is) used to do a lot of lifting, painting, stuff like that, and I used to work in the laundry near the ships. We're both from Whitby, and we met because we like to run."

I deliver another of my expressions (a simple one – just *polite surprise* – but formed with unusual finesse and precision), and she's encouraged to expand.

"Oh yes," she says. "I'm very fit. You must have seen me running at the Lookout – six times round the park every day?"

I confess I'd never noticed.

"Yes. Rye too. We used to run and run, keeping fit and healthy together, all round the town. We used to run in the country, up the hill to Staithes, Boulby and the cliffs, Hinderwell and all round the hills there. Running, running, running, running – as if our feet turned the world. We got really sweaty..." She stops for a moment and her eyes lose focus... (I can see she's remembering something – perhaps something to do with sweat) ...but the pause lasts only an instant. "Then he said we should get married. And that was it really. I was twenty; he was two years older. Rye's family lived in Bedale, so he moved in with me and my mum and dad in Whitby. Rye heard about the school, and we moved to the Lookout eight years ago. We were happy..."

I point out the fact they'd been married for ten years and inquire why no children are evident.

"We do want children," she replies, "but it's not time yet. We've been very careful..."

I ponder for a few seconds, wondering if I should ask about the precise nature of this *"being careful"*, but decide to mind my own business. I do, however, point out that time is marching on, and they'd better get breeding before life's twilight sets in.

"Thank you, sir." She smiles, taking my words as a promise *(Thou shalt give birth to a son...)*. "God bless you."

In the brief stillness that follows, moans can be heard drifting from above, as of someone in pain. I hear the padding feet again and conclude that the nude woman has got the better of fit Zachariah Ousby.

I point at shy little Fanny Kirkbride, the smallest (and presumably youngest) of the dairymaids, and she reddens with embarrassment. *Come, come, you sweet little thing*, says my expression (pouting lips are involved with that one). She cowers back a bit in her seat, smiling coyly. It's captivating, and I begin to salivate.

"I'm just a chimney sweep's gal," she twinkles modestly.

I display *surprised curiosity* (large eyes, tilted head – otherwise mostly eyebrows) and invite her to continue.

"I'm a bit like 'gals at 'school, I s'pose," she says. "I worked wi' me mam in 'work'ouse kitchen at Middlesbrough. Me dad ran off when I were young. I liked to climb, and went cavin' when I could – which wa'n't very often. You can see 'ow smaall I am."

I tell her, yes, I can see that – indeed, it has always struck me. She's like a cuddly doll. (My Wickedness, speaking close to my ear, suggests she might make an ideal hot water bottle.)

"Well, I took to climbin' up 'work'ouse chimneys – for fun. And then me mam said there might be a bit o' money in it and hired me out to 'chimney sweep. It were good – like cavin' – and I done it every day.

I went round wi' 'im in 'is cart. Then one day 'e just keeled over and died – and I was by meself again." She pauses. "I couldn't go back to me mother – she'd died too. So I 'ad no-one."

I'm sorry to hear that and issue my sympathy.

"That was when I started to look round for a job. 1756 it were. That's when I come to 'Lookout.

I do a quick calculation and express surprise. She couldn't have been more than twelve at the time.

"Oh, no," she replies. "I were eighteen. I'm nearly twenty-eight now."

Again, I'm astonished. She looks no more than twenty-two. I tell her so.

She smiles, pleased. "No, no. I just look younger. I guess it's coal dust keeps me skin young."

I ask if she'd ever been up the chimneys at the Lookout.

"Not just 'chimneys," she replies. "All 'secret places too. All 'secret passages no-one knows about, all 'hidden rooms." She pauses and looks around her at the other women. "Did you know there's a second cellar?"

We're all enthralled, and gasp.

"There is," she says. "I'm the only one who knows about it. There's a passage in 'wall be'ind 'kitchen. You think at first it ends in a blank wall, but if you push on 'top o' 'wall, a panel opens up below. Be'ind that panel there's a stone staircase that leads down, and down. Seventy-six steps." She speaks slowly, nodding, aware that we're captivated. "There's a second cellar – underneath the one everyone knows about – a *great* big room, all black and damp…"

"What's in it?" asks Neva, eyes on stalks, hair erect.

Fanny grins like a demon, holds us all in silent thrall, then hisses, "Coffins!"

Eyes widen in shock; hands fly to mouths in horror. Fanny watches for a couple of seconds, then bursts into laughter. The women, realising they've been taken for a ride, gasp with relief and join in Fanny's mirth, hands at their hearts, calming themselves. I watch them, wondering if Fanny has hidden a grain of truth in a tall story. My curiosity will have to wait.

"Can I 'ave a look up your chimney?" she says, like an enthusiastic medical student, nodding at the drawing room fireplace.

I'm mealy-mouthed at first, hadn't anticipated the question. The chimneys have never been swept in sixty years. I throw up my hands and raise my eyebrows in an improvised gesture of *Help Yourself*.

"Great!" she says, leaping up. "I'll 'ave to get me chimney-urchin gear on. It's in me bag. You'll prob'ly want to look away while I strip off."

I reluctantly withdraw and stand by the window. There's a lot of commotion behind me, and I hear the other women giggling and fussing, helping Fanny with her things.

The sun's still shining. I scan left and right, looking for Theo and Sukey, but they're not in sight – must be on the other side of the house. I turn, hurry from the room (keeping the flashes of pink in the extreme corner of my eye), and dash to the kitchen window. Ethel remains in her accustomed place near the apple tree, but Birdie is lying on the ground, unmoving, her body sprawled face down. She's probably dead at last, and I briefly reflect that it couldn't have happened on a nicer day. I spy Sukey and Theo strolling arm-in-arm at two o'clock, moving steadily towards the garden path.

Shouts of "Ready!" reel me back to the drawing room. There's Fanny, spangly-eyed and eager to discover new worlds. She's raggedly dressed in a dark blue jacket and breeches that look like they're made of sacking, the ensemble topped off with a cheeky little peaked cap. Her feet are bare.

"I'm inflamed with excitement!" she cries, energy popping. I smile, indicate the vertical shaft's gaping mouth, and wish her good luck. She steps to the fireplace, ducks her head into the chimney, takes a grip with both hands and braces her pretty pink tootsies on the brickwork. Then she's gone. Leafy, Neva, Delia and Flossie break into spontaneous applause and shout encouragement: "Go, Fanny! Yipyipyip! Don't break a leg! Hurrah!"

We listen for a while. A few bits of black stuff fall into the hearth, and the scrambling sounds fade until only silence remains. Delia crouches, sticks her head up the chimney, and shouts, "How is it?" But there's no reply. We sit and wait – glance politely at each other and listen for noises from the pipe.

Nothing.

I offer cakes and biscuits, then go to the kitchen

and freshen the tea. I look through the window as the kettle boils. Birdie is still dead; Sukey and Theo are out of sight; Ethel sits, carved, martyr-like, her wimple tight and severe, entirely concealing her grey head.

Ten minutes have passed by the time I return to the drawing room. Neva is on her hands and knees, peering up the chimney.

"Fanny?"

We listen, but there's not a whisper. I set down the tea things and hand round the cups.

"Do you think she's in trouble?" asks Leafy.

"No," Flossie replies. "She's fit as a fiddle, and she's done this a thousand times."

"Why doesn't she reply then?" asks Leafy.

"Don't know," Flossie answers. "P'raps her mouth is full of dirt."

A few heads nod. Yes, that's the likely reason.

The house is very quiet. There's no sound from Rye or the nude woman. I speculate as to what might be occurring upstairs. Who is the victor? What might victory entail? Why is it all so deathly silent?

"We could go outside and watch," Neva suggests. "She might be out on the roof already."

They nod their heads and mutter that it's a good plan.

"I'll stay here," Neva suggests, "in case she comes down."

A couple of minutes later, we're standing at the rear of the garden, looking up at the roof. The chimney pots are all narrow, and it occurs to me that even little Fanny might have a problem squeezing through one of those. Still, I assure myself, she's a professional. It's not for me to ignorantly speculate.

It's turned out to be a lovely day – clear blue sky, a few wispy clouds high up. A pair of blue tits flit about; a hare races across the field in the distance.

Sukey and Theo pass by. "Good afternoon, sir," Sukey greets me, raising a hand and smiling sweetly. I check my watch; it is indeed after noon. We watch the couple as they continue their rotation.

Flossie lifts her skirts and begins to run in circles, quicker and quicker, panting, sweating, leaping over obstacles as if she's a horse in a steeplechase.

"Wheeee!" she pipes. "C'mon! Join in! Nice big garden – keep fit!" She repeatedly pogos on the spot, hooting enthusiastically, before charging off again. Delia looks doubtfully at me; I look doubtfully at Delia. No-one takes up Flossie's invitation.

Fifteen minutes pass. No sign of Fanny.

"Do you think she's gone for good?" asks Leafy.

"No," Delia replies. "She'll come out – top or bottom."

I suggest we have a picnic while we wait. The ladies leap up and down, clapping their hands with excitement.

Back inside, I first ask Neva if there's been any sign of activity. Receiving a negative response, I stand in the stairwell and call Rye's name. No answer – complete stillness. I cry out for the nude woman, but my shout is consumed in the vast cavern of lofty spaces. The air seems alive in the house today, as if the place has breath of its own.

I prepare a fine feast for my visitors and carry the food and drink into the garden on several trays. The process occupies more than half an hour. Sukey and Theo pause in their perambulations to partake with us, and I wonder if I might coax Ethel to do the same. I walk to her spot, but she's sitting motionless, waiting for God to issue instructions.

Birdie's still there, and I examine her body at close range. Her eyes are bulging and bloodshot, her mouth open, black tongue protruding grotesquely as if she's been strangled. She's not breathing; definitely dead. A spider, fat and black, hurries out of her mouth. Are there any more in there?

I pass through the house on my way back to the others, checking with Neva. She's a good girl, watching like this, and I reward her with a pork pie, mustard, and a bottle of lemonade. She's thrilled.

The party at the rear of the house seems to have forgotten about Fanny. "Oh, sorry!" says Delia, "we weren't watching. I'm sure she'd have shouted if she'd got out."

"She's probably lost," offers Leafy. "Don't worry about it."

"I expect she's gone forever," says Sukey. "Never mind. Worse things happen at sea."

I look up at the mute chimney pots. Flossie charges past me at speed, gasping, slick with exertion's slime.

They set up a rota to relieve Neva, watching the mouth of the drawing room chimney in case little Fanny drops out. But she doesn't.

We eat, drink, tell stories, laugh; Delia sings a dirty song, and it sets off a string of risky jokes (Leafy doesn't contribute to those but sits red-faced with embarrassment).

I enjoy the cooling evening with my milky nymphs till the sun begins to sink.

"We should be on our way," Neva suggests.

It's been a nice day. Pretty ladies.

"Oh well," says Delia, standing at the door, the first in line to say goodbye. "No use cryin' over spilt milk."

There's a sudden tremendous commotion on the stairs, and a middle-aged woman in a dark red dress comes screaming down, runs across the hall, tears through the knot of milkmaids at the front door, and escapes into the evening. I watch her rapidly departing figure with some confusion – and then remember who she is.

"My God!" says Delia as the woman dissolves into the distance. "Was that Stella?"

No, not Stella, I tell them – it was Miss Shadow.

Rye bangs noisily down the staircase. His shirt is bloody; there's a meat cleaver in his chest. I express horror, and the women scream.

"This?" he says, gripping the handle of the weapon. "Just a flesh wound. Look..." He jumps up and down, stands on his hands and performs cartwheels on the garden path. "Fit as a fiddle."

I ask him about the nude woman.

"Nude woman?" He frowns. "Didn't see one. I kept my peepers peeled all day, but there was only her in the red frock. Nasty bit of work, she was."

I'm both disappointed and glad that he didn't discover my lady.

Delia is standing arms outstretched, eyes closed, lips pursed expectantly; so I scrunch her again in my embrace, lick my lips and splatter her with a kiss, repeating the process one by one with the three other women. The procedure occupies just over half an hour. Rye stands by patiently – I hope he's not waiting for his turn. Finally, the group saunters away down the front path.

The sky is clear, but the light is fading. I pay one more visit to Ethel Coombs. She doesn't acknowledge my presence. Birdie Wade is nowhere to be seen. I ask after her but, predictably, get no reply.

Into the drawing room once more before the night. I kneel in the hearth, look up the black inverted pit of the chimney, and call Fanny's name. My voice echoes remotely in the infinity of undiscoverable worlds and is lost.

Time for bed.

2.

Clouds
John Sykes and Cornelius East

I wake in the pink dawn light, surface from sleep gradually, recall I'm a living thing as the seconds of awareness build into something resembling continuous consciousness.

I've seen Kate. The experience seemed real, but now I think it must have been a dream. I was in Scrawby church, sitting quietly in one of the pews. It was day, but the light was dull, grey-blue, pale. There was no sound at first, then a soft click, like a tiny bit of grit dropping to the stone floor from somewhere above. A mouse, I guess, or a bird, flicking something through a hole in the roof. Despite the stillness, the place must be full of life: nesting birds, mice, insects, spiders. I listened for the cooing of pigeons, doves, but didn't hear anything.

The ghosts were all there, more than fifty of them, sitting motionless as Fuzzy had seen them. I twisted around in my seat and looked at their grey, unsmiling faces. The movement of my body made the pew squeak, the sound shocking in the place's ancient silence. But none of them showed any awareness of it; their eyes stared straight ahead into the centuries yet to come.

I turned to my right, and there she was, not four

feet from me, wrapped in her cape, hood down, staring sightlessly as the others did, her impossible hair displacing the reality around her head, gathering all the universes into one awareness. I thought of Samson, but he was just a boy compared with her, the pillars of the temple nothing more than tubes of paper.

She didn't see me. Her expression remained fixed, impassive. I moved close to her, reached out and touched her arm, but she didn't move. I pressed against her and breathed softly onto her cheek, not expecting a response. But I was wrong. She turned her head and looked directly at me, her big hazel eyes like pits of time, terrifying.

I'd thought she lived in me, but now I see it's the other way round. She surrounds and encloses me, allows my crumbling universe to exist within her eternity.

How could it have been any other way?

It's frigid in my bed, so I get up and go downstairs.

"Morning!" A man's voice in the drawing room. I put my head round the door and find John Sykes sitting in front of a roaring fire. He raises a hand in greeting. "I let myself in. Hope you don't mind. The door was open."

I look beyond him at the blaze and think of poor Fanny. Ah well, it's too late to worry now. I ask John if he'd like some tea, but he raises his cup, indicating he's already made a pot, and invites me to sit with him. I pull my dressing gown close, sit on the sofa opposite, and watch him pour.

"I've a bone to pick with you," he says.

I express dismay, although I can guess what he wants to complain about.

"I was already dead when the story began," he explains. "I had a lot to say – was looking forward to saying it – and the first thing that happens is my own bloody funeral. Explain yourself, man!"

I offer a gesture of sympathy but cast my defence along the lines that a story has to begin somewhere. In any case, I tell him, it wasn't *his* story but that of his great-granddaughter.

"Yes," he says, "I see that, but you've got an awful lot of scene-setting stuff about my girl Hazel – and her daughter Nara. What about me? There are things I know that were lost with me – that can't now be part of the tale."

I sit back, frowning, and wait for more.

"And my lovely Scarlet? She could have told you a thing or two. But she's in the ground fourteen years before you begin."

I start to feel guilty, thoughtless. I've never been able to do anything right. Whatever decision I take, it's always the wrong one. It's true – I could have started the thread a few generations earlier, could have gone right back to Anne White – or even the centuries, the millennia, that preceded her. But I halt my fretting and point out to him that there are many more stories to come. Willa's, for instance – little Willa, given to the priest by her own mother so she could live, eat, and have a roof over her head. How far back is that? Seventh century? Certainly before the Vikings came.

"Ah, but you see," says John, tapping his nose, "I know things relevant to your tale, that you can't now use."

I demand to know what, for instance.

He leans forward. "Scarlet's chair."

I tilt my head and display *curious but uncomprehending*.

"You know," he continues animatedly. "What they all think is Scarlet's chair – the big one that sits in the parlour at Vine Cottage – the one with handles, so it can be moved easily. You've got plans for that in the future, I bet." He peers at me, eyebrows raised, and nods. He's pleased with himself – thinks he's got me by the curlies. He probably has, too. I wait for the blow to fall.

"Aha! You see?" He wags his finger at me. "Well, it's not Scarlet's chair at all. That chair was made by James White for his daughter Daisy – Scarlet's mother. It's Daisy's chair." He fixes me with a stare sharp as a rapier and delivers the final blow: "And it's made from the wood of Anne White's gallows."

The single word, *shit*, lights up in my mind, in letters big as houses, fifty feet off the ground.

"You didn't know that, did you?" he grins, and I admit that I did not. "Well, the secret's gone now, and no-one will ever know exactly what that chair is."

I feel a considerable degree of irritation and ask him why the information was not passed down in his family.

"Scarlet thought the truth too morbid – to have something like that in the house. So we never told Hazel." He raises his eyebrows, shakes his head. "She never knew."

I'm disappointed. I don't know what to say. It's a nice little story that would have added an extra thong to the narrative's cat o' nine tails. But he's right. The truth is out of reach now. And no-one will ever know.

We talk a while longer, then he pulls his pipe from his pocket and asks to smoke. "Do you mind?"

I tell him I'd welcome the tobacco haze – it gives the room an ambience. I've been thinking of hunting down my old pipes. I used to smoke decades ago. It was a relaxing thing to do, and Kate's enthusiasm for it has made me hanker after it again. God knows where the equipment is though – I certainly won't find it today.

John lights up, and the room begins to cloud with memories. "Chess?" he asks.

I like the idea and dig out my old set. I haven't played for more than forty years – no-one seems to care for it these days; everyone's too distracted with nothings and zeros and pointlessnesses and crap.

"I used to play chess with Cornelius," says John. "We'd sit in the garden and play in the summer evenings." He puffs, remembering, his eyes far away as I set up the pieces. "Cornelius never met Scarlet. You should have seen my Scarlet. She was the beauty of the farm. Ah, how I miss her. Dead at forty-nine; wasted away in the last few months…" He's lost for a moment, gathers himself and goes on. "Oswin knew her, though. I'm grateful for that. Oswin married my Hazel in 1718, a year before Scarlet passed away, so we had a few months together at Vine Cottage, all four of us. Happy times." He looks at me, takes a huge draw on his pipe, blows out the smoke in an extravagant fog, and goes on: "Anyway, enough about me. You must be bored. Let's get down to business. I haven't played chess since I died."

We settle down and concentrate. He beats me easily; I'm out of practice. I offer him a glass of whisky, and he accepts. We settle into a second game, and he slaughters me again. He sits back in his chair and refreshes his pipe. "I thought you said you were a good player."

I apologise and tell him I was better before I was twenty.

The drawing room door creaks open, and I peer over my shoulder. It's Cornelius East.

"Bugger me!" John exclaims. He rests his pipe on the tabletop, rises, and opens his arms.

"John!" Cornelius beams, hastening forward, embracing him. "How wonderful to see you again after all these years." Both men shed a few tears. I wait for them to disengage. Cornelius wipes his cheeks, looks at me and explains, "I let myself in."

I tell him the door's never locked. John reseats himself, and I pull up a chair for the unexpected guest.

"I've been smoking," says John to the parson. "Do you mind if I go on? I mean, I know some people think it's bad for you."

"Not at all," says Cornelius. "Puff away. Reminds me of the old days."

The tobacco's aroma has infiltrated my senses. My own pipe can't be too far away, and John has someone else to keep him company, so this is a good time to search. I'm in the act of rising from my seat when Cornelius catches my attention and asks, "Nude woman?"

I'm taken off-guard and don't instantly grasp what he means.

"Nude woman," he repeats. "I think I heard one padding about upstairs as I walked through your hall."

I'm relieved, understanding. I'd thought for a moment that he was asking for one, as one might ask for a biscuit, or a cup of tea. I haven't heard the nude woman since yesterday, so am warmed to hear that she's still there. I reply in the affirmative.

Cornelius nods. "I thought so. Never had one in the parsonage, not in all these years." His nodding head changes direction and gives a little shake. "Never once." He looks pensive, and I sense a great regret in him. I smile and offer pork pie and cake. The eyes of both men come alive. Pork pie and cake is a pretty effective short-term substitute for nude women.

I leave the two men playing chess, step out into the hall, and look up into the maze of platforms and staircases, holding my breath, listening hard. Yes, there she is; I hear her footfalls. Peering way up almost to the limit of my vision, I pick out a glimpse of something – a leg, an arm perhaps, and the fingers of a hand briefly gripping a bannister rail. I call up, and the noises cease for a moment as if the nude woman hears me. There's no reply, and the supple padding resumes, hastening I know not where, wherefrom or for what purpose.

John's reminiscing has conjured a sense of loss in me. I wonder if I should visit the caverns beneath the house – wander down a few steps. Is now the time? There's the door – to the right of the kitchen, set beneath the lowest flight of stairs. I step over to it, take hold of the handle and pull, instantly aware of the chill of the past. The darkness within is unwelcoming. I change my mind and click the door shut.

It takes only a few minutes to gather food and drink for Cornelius and John. They mutter thanks when I deliver the refreshment but hardly lift their eyes from the game in which they're involved. It's quiet in the smoke-filled room, the two men lost in their strategy. The only sound is the crackle of the fire. Again, I think of poor Fanny. If she's caught somewhere up the pipe, she'll be well cooked by now.

I leave the two men by themselves. Sadness has crept up, so I step into the garden, wander over to the apple tree, and sit on the bench with Ethel. She doesn't react to my proximity, doesn't speak.

There's movement away to the left, behind the

house, and I'm surprised to see Theo and Sukey come into view, still on their widdershins circuit. Have they been there all night? When I judge they're within shouting range, I call and inquire.

Sukey waves. "We can't seem to break away," she says. "It's as if we're in orbit. There must be a kind of attraction in the house; you know – a centre of gravity."

I find the notion reassuring but am concerned for their wellbeing.

"We'll probably die one day," Theo calls back, "but we're happy enough for now. Perhaps the house will fall down first."

"Ha!" laughs Ethel. I scowl at her.

The satellites pass on their way.

The evening is warm, sizzling with the ecstasy of grasshoppers. John, Cornelius and I sit outside in the pink sunset, drinking gin and looking over the fields west of the house.

"How long's it been?" asks Cornelius.

"Thirty-three years," John replies. "Doesn't seem possible."

The parson's eyes slip away from the garden and turn within his memory. "Those were lovely days, happy days." He pauses. "I'm nearly sixty-six. I wonder how much time is left for me?" He waits a few seconds, then looks at John. "How old were you? I can't quite remember."

"When I died?"

"Mm."

"Seventy-six. You've got plenty of time."

"I wonder," Cornelius muses.

Crows cackle in the trees nearby.

"Dying's easy," says John. "Watching someone die – someone you love – that's hard."

Cornelius reaches out and rests his hand on John's knee. "Good friend," he says.

We sit in silence a while, John smoking his pipe, Sukey and Theo on their circuit behind us. The sky reddens.

John removes his pipe from his mouth and leans forward, peering into the distance. "There she is," he says.

I follow the direction of his gaze and see a woman, far away, walking towards us.

"It's my Scarlet," John murmurs.

Cornelius squints, locates the figure. "Scarlet…" he echoes in wonder.

She's tall and thin, like a mirage, far away. Her image flickers in the evening air. She's ambling towards us, constantly advancing.

But she'll never arrive.

3.

Alfred Bentley – Alan Blake
Bip and Eve – the village
Alvina and Rodney
Under the house
Seph

I became aware in the soft glow of pre-dawn and realised that time had stopped. It wouldn't move again until I said so. I had to get up.

The house was silent. I stood on the landing outside my bedroom door, cocked my head and listened, but there were no padding feet. Perhaps she sleeps.

It was dark outside, with only a hint of blue glow on the eastern horizon. Fresh, chilly. The grass was damp under my bare feet. I could just pick out the dewdrops decorating the spiderwebs, shining in the light from the kitchen window.

The bench by the apple tree was empty. I wonder what Ethel would do if she arrived at her plinth in the early morning to find it occupied by me, a bastard bloody man? Would she turn round in fury and stomp back to the house? I must try it one day.

I waited a while, curious to see if Sukey and Theo persisted on their course. They didn't appear – but *something* was circling the house. I noticed the eyes first: six tiny mirrors glowing dully pink in the gloom. Then the figures became visible – three creeping, skulking, bent things – shrivelled, cowled, clutching each other. The smell of decay wafted off them, the stink of centuries. They glared at me as they stumbled past, hissing, hating.

The sky was brighter – almost dawn.

AMOR DORMIENTI

I was standing in the arcade of Vivianne's tomb at the Lookout, staring at the sea, as Kate liked to do. I glanced at the spot where she pissed that morning – her Sermon to the Gods – but it was dry. The wind had kissed away the evidence of her.

"They've all gone."

Alfred Bentley's voice startled me. I turned, and there he was, standing a few feet away.

"It's over," he explained. "The Lookout's finished. The last ones moved out nearly a week ago."

I was surprised to see him smoking what looked like a cigar. The effect was stark, daring, like the emergence of a new fashion. It suited his dignified moustachioed rotundity. He noticed my expression, took the thing from his mouth, looked at it and said, "What, this? It's a cigarro – from Spain. I have my contacts," he winked at me, "and I prefer it to my pipe." He took a puff and added, "Looks good, no? Attracts the women."

I agreed it lent him a certain uniqueness, then asked him why there was no Mrs Bentley.

"There was once," he replied. "Twenty years ago, and

more. Ran off with my best friend – bastard."

I offered my condolences and told him he was a good-looking man and could attract a wife easily enough even now, in his middle fifties.

"Maybe," he puffed. "I'd need to lose a bit of weight. I used to be fit, but I've lost it now."

I disagreed and reassured him that fat men are the best.

He snorted, looked askance at me and concurred. "You're right."

The first golden drop of sun appeared above the sea's horizon and cast a narrow pathway of lantern light across the water's surface.

Alfred continued. "But I was never on the prowl for quiff after she left." He drew on his cigarro again, breathed in the smoke and blew it out through his nose. "Not like that, in any case."

I asked him if he was of the other persuasion.

He laughed. "Me? No, not a bit."

He looked at me intently, wondering if he should say more. I saw the indecision on his face and raised my eyebrows, encouraging him to go on.

"It was a good job here." He sighed and bowed his head against the rising sun, saddened. "I liked to look at the girls. It was like having charge of a box of sweets you could never eat. Delicious, the anticipation – aching." He paused, looked at me again, then went on hurriedly. "I never took one. God! Course I didn't. I'd never have hurt them. I loved them, all of them." Another long pause. "To think what that bastard did with them..."

I looked at the sea, the golden sun inching higher, lighting the sky like honey, drop by drop.

Alfred's tobacco smoke had vanished. He was no longer there. Alan Blake, blacksmith, stood in his place, looking anxious, twisting his hat in his hands, waiting for me to ask him. I didn't do so, but it was clear he had something to get off his chest, so I stared at him till it popped out of its own accord.

"You know," he said. "You're the only one who does."

I gave no reply but waited quietly to catch the story he was about to throw me.

"It was her tits." His gaze fell to the floor, and he replaced his hat on his head. "It was always tits with me. I was a tit man, first and always. You've seen Chastity, my wife. Lovely woman. I always loved her; still do. Wonderful bosom."

The silence of regret drifted around him as he gathered his thoughts. I sensed the weight of his burden.

He breathed deep and went on, speaking slowly, pausing every so often to recall – to re-imagine the colours, the textures, the warmth. "Annie Smyth was one of the first girls here. She arrived just before Christmas 1755, sixteen years old – ripe – juicy as a peach. The Christmas service marked the opening of the chapel – the first event. I noticed her then, in the candlelight, dress cut low... I can see her now." He looked up, eyes glowing in the sun, moist with the memory. "She was a beauty! Only a few girls were here in those days – they were still being gathered.

And there were many staff appointments yet to be made, so the place wasn't as busy as it later became. I came across her once or twice – by accident – and I could never keep my eyes off her... you know."

He was heavy with guilt. I waited for him to continue.

"She wasn't so innocent," he grated. "She knew what I wanted. And I think she liked me. It was something about the heat of the forge – the dirt and grime – that attracted her. Took me months to get my courage up. I said I'd show her round the smithy." He waited a few seconds, then muttered, "She knew what that meant." Another pause. "Chastity liked to visit Scarborough one Saturday each month to see her friends and do a bit of shopping. Barney was five years old then. Sometimes she'd take him with her. I told Anne to come that day."

He shut his eyes and sighed. Tears formed and squeezed out, ran down his cheeks. He tried to control himself, sniffed, stifled his sobs. It was more than half a minute before he could go on. "That was it. We both knew it was going to happen." He swallowed. "I took her upstairs straightaway, unwrapped her..." He wiped his eyes, pressing with his fingers, then shook his head, paused, and sighed once more, remembering. "It was like the command of Fate – like something that had to take place so the world could go on."

He stopped speaking and leaned back against the tomb. I was unsure if he'd continue, so I watched the lightening sea again, listened to the waves on the shore, scanned the broch on the clifftop. Gulls wheeled and cried, lifted on the wind.

"She was a devil in bed," said Alan. "I mean, Chastity was wonderful – still is. But Chastity's a clean girl, daughter of an archdeacon."

I hadn't been aware of that. I raised my eyebrows in surprise, simultaneously stifling my amusement at his assumption that the daughter of a cleric couldn't also be "a devil in bed."

"Oh, yes," he went on. "Chastity Reynolds was her maiden name. I used to work in Lincoln; that's where we met. 1746 it was. God knows what her father saw in me, but he didn't raise any objections. She told him she loved me. Me! A common smith! She was twenty-four; I was twenty-seven. She was gorgeous. And she had the most glorious tits I'd ever seen. So we got wed, and she moved in with me. Her father gave us a fair bit of financial support – still does. The house was always nice, the food was always good... She can cook, Chastity." He shook his head, despairing at himself. "God! What was I thinking?"

I asked him what went wrong.

"Nothing went wrong," he replied. "Life was good. It took a while for Barney to come along. That was 1752. We'd been trying for five years. There were no more bairns – just the one. But we were happy. Then I saw the notice for this place, and we all moved up here. It seemed like a good idea – an idyllic life in the countryside by the sea. And it *was* lovely. That was 1755." He paused, took a couple of steps forward, and leant on one of the pillars supporting the arcade. "We'd been married more than seven years when we arrived here. You know what they say about people who've been married seven years. It's supposed to be the time when heads turn. When I saw Anne Smyth, she reminded me of Chastity, but younger." He took another step forward and looked out at the water. "I felt guilty straight away, that first time – as soon as it couldn't be undone. But every month she'd come back – and I'd want her to come back. She was like fire – and there's a thrill playing with fire. I saw her once a month for ten months. Every time was going to be the last time – that's what I told myself. But I couldn't resist her. She was the temptress of the school. All the men said so. You should have heard some of the comments. Each and every one of them would have given an eye to have had what I had. And none of them ever knew. Eventually, Anne went off to London – and now we know what was waiting for her." He grimaced. "And that makes me feel like shit. I couldn't even protect her."

I asked him if Chastity knew about Anne, and he answered instantly. "No. Absolutely not. I never told her – she doesn't know. She thinks I've been a good and faithful husband. And I *have* been – apart from *her*. Annie left the school nine years ago, and I never saw her again. She'll be twenty-seven now. I wonder where she is, what she's doing." He removed his hat and began twisting it again. "I love Chastity, and my boy. I *can't* tell her – never be able to. It would break her, and I don't want that." He shook his head. "No, it's my burden. I have to carry it for the rest of my life. It weighs me down every day. The shame in my heart – it's almost more than I can bear."

I wanted to reach out in understanding but doubted my sympathy would give him any consolation. I suggested that maybe his remorse was the payment he had to make for his actions.

"Of course it is," he answered. "I try to be a good man." He looked directly at me. "Listen. Only you, me, and Anne Smyth know about this. Can we keep it that way?"

I assured him that his secret was secure.

"Good," he nodded. "Thank you. I'm glad I told you."

The sun's orb rested fully on the world's rim. There were no more words – only the wash of waves on the beach. Alan had gone.

The top floor of the watermill. Daylight leaks in around the closed window shutters, narrow shafts of gold picking out gliding dust motes in the forgotten past.

It stinks; the place is filled with flies. I know he's hanging there; I'm aware of his sagging black shape, dangling on the rope beneath the pulley wheel. But I don't want to look. The mill is full of whispering voices, murmuring souls in perpetual torment, trapped in the dark for centuries.

As my eyes become accustomed to the gloom, I see the skulking thing – things: the three brothers, cowering in the corner, hiding among the cobwebs, spiders running over their cowled faces, filthy with the grime of time. They watch me silently with their dull pink eyes, drooling. I can't see their spittle as it oozes oil-like on their withered lips, but I can hear the thick drops splash every few seconds into the pools of slime at their feet.

The air in the room is heavy – dense with hate. An infinity of cruelty is compressed into this space, an abyss of evil.

The clamour rises, the voices cry out with greater anguish, deeper suffering.

Can you hear them?

I stand on Watermill Lane and look down at the boarded-up building. It's bright daylight and the birds are singing, but the mill's chill fingers creep up into the road. I'm deep in thought and don't see the two women approach.

"Hello," says a voice. "Fancy bumping into you here, of all places."

I look to my right and am astonished to see Anne Pringle and Eve Miller. Anne is dressed in pale blue, Eve in a soft brown that reflects the sun's light. Both carry parasols. I greet them by name and hug them simultaneously. I hadn't previously imagined myself standing next to Anne and am surprised to find how statuesque and startling she is. Her dark brown hair is rich and full, and I notice for the first time how lovely her eyes are – big and blue. She's about five feet, eight inches tall. How old is she now? I work it out... almost the same age as Kate, of course – just a few months younger – seventeen on September 21st (she thinks her birthday's the 16th – but we know it's not. She'll find out one day...).

She's watching me – notices how impressed I am. "You always thought of me as Kate's friend, didn't you? Never thought I might have a life of my own."

It's true. She's always travelled such a close orbit around Kate that her own essence has been obscured in the brilliance. But here she stands exposed, out of the glare, and I can appreciate the landscape of her own being in the detail it deserves. I reassure her that her tale is coming. It's all planned: Anne Pringle – origin, life and loves.

She raises her eyebrows. "Loves? That'll make a change. And you'd better stop calling me Anne. You've got enough Annes already. No-one calls me Anne. It's Bip. Call me Bip, like everyone else."

I apologise. She reaches out and squeezes my hand. I always like it when my people do that, particularly the women; it reassures me that I'm not a waste of oxygen.

Eve comes forward. She's about four inches shorter than Bip and about twice her age, with thick, curly brown hair a shade lighter than the younger woman's. "Hey! I'm here too. Lettice, Eleanor and Denise all have stories, but not me. Why not? Look." She spreads out her arms and spins around. "I'm a pretty fine object. I fizz, and I'm supposed to be the captain of the housemistresses. But you haven't coloured me in."

I'm not sure that's entirely fair and point out a

few choice moments that have slipped her memory. But I do hear her pleas and convince her that she's cherished, like the others, and not to be left behind. This saga has a long, long way to go yet. It's early days.

"You better remember," she says, narrowing her eyes and directing an impressive fingernail at me.

I tell them I'm surprised to see them both here, close to the farm.

"You've forgotten," says Bip. "Look."

She points beyond the watermill to the field in the distance – south of the manor house and above Egton.

Of course.

I see the new buildings going up, many of them complete. Even at this distance, I can pick out a few people moving about.

"The Lookout's in the past," says Bip. "We live in Cappleman Village now. Kate's magic land."

I ask how it's going, but Eve cuts in. "Now, now. That would be telling. That story's to come. Isn't it…?"

The nude woman sprints past right outside my bedroom door, drawing me partly awake. I notice the dawn light creeping through the curtains and listen as her hurrying feet disappear up the stairs. Counting her footfalls is like counting sheep. I get to 236 before I nod off again.

I enter Cappleman Village at the western edge. It's too early for most people to be awake, so I should get a good look at how things are shaping up without worrying anyone. I don't want to infiltrate their world too deeply. Perhaps I'll live here among them one day. That would be amazing. I'd love that.

I walk forward. The village is bigger than I'd imagined. Hugh's done a superb job; he's thought of everything. I know Alex helped, and wonder who else had a hand in it. I pass a few early risers and raise my hat to them. Some look at me, puzzled. They think they know me, but can't place who I am. It's best that way – unless they come to my house.

Someone's singing through an open window. I pause and listen. It's a cheerful voice, a woman. I nod in recognition. It's Mary Acker, probably working at something – ironing, maybe – I don't know. It's nice to hear her. Lovely lady. If she's singing to herself at sunrise, things must be happy – for her, at least.

There's a laundry. That was good thinking. Mary Stafford is hanging out washing in the yard. I raise my hat and call, "Good morning."

She peers, squints, but I can see she doesn't recognise me. "Good day, sir," she says.

"Looks like it'll be a fine one," I throw back.

"Let's hope so."

"Family well?"

I wonder if Crispin is still here, with his wife, Winnie. It's possible they've moved away, but I guess the others still work in the laundry: Mary's husband Michael, and their daughters, Beryl, Barbara and Sylvia.

Mary's frowning. "Do I know you, sir?"

I've gone too far – she's worried. "No," I reply. "Not Directly. I'm just passing through before I wake. Trying not to draw attention to myself."

She nods, not reassured. "We're all fine here, sir. Thanks for asking."

I raise my hat and move on.

There's a large building under construction behind the laundry – I notice it as I continue down the main street. I walk to the entrance, try the door, but it's locked. Too early. What is it? I circuit, peering through glassless windows, standing on bits of masonry to spy over unfinished walls. Looks like a bathhouse. What a fantastic idea! I knew Hugh had an interest in the Romans – grew up with it, fascinated by their history and the artefacts they left behind. I suppose this is his enthusiasm manifesting in stone. Good for him! I wonder how they achieved it; pulling water off the Esk, I guess, and passing it back downriver. Is it heated? Bet it is. Fascinating!

I retrace my steps and continue my little wander, noting the library, a building I reckon might be a schoolhouse, the infirmary…

The door to the last squeaks open, and a young woman lets a cat out into the street. She's in her nightdress and leaps back inside when she sees me. It's Nana Hall. I smile, warmed. Does her presence here so early in the morning mean that she and Hollis…? I hope so. She deserves to be happy.

The morning lightens further as I stroll on. Here's the inn, opposite the green. It's called *The*

Broomstick. Is that a joke? I like the name. There's a paddock nearby. I count five mares, all of whom I know: Athena, Nemesis, Aphrodite, Artemis, Hera. I step over to the fence and watch them fondly, particularly Athena, Kate's favourite.

"Keen on horses, sir?"

I turn round and greet Stanley Tanner. "I don't know much about them, to be honest," I admit. "But I know these five."

"You know them?" he asks, perplexed.

"Of course," I answer.

He's curious. "Did you visit the school?"

I'm not sure precisely how to answer the question and flounder for a moment before adopting the easiest response. "Yes."

"A friend of…Jacob?"

I pause again, then look at him and say, "No. Not exactly."

He turns his attention to the animals. "There was a sixth, but she was taken."

"Demeter," I return.

"That's right," he says, eyebrows raised, realising I do genuinely know the horses.

I'm curious about Stanley. I have a little knowledge of Kipp and Nolly but not so much about Stanley. "Are you happy here in the village?" I ask him.

"I am," he says. "It's a dream. I've been pretty fortunate really – all my life. Always worked with horses. Cared for them, trained them, ridden them, raced them."

"Where are you from?"

"Newmarket originally – worked at the racecourse. My father too, and his father."

"Bit of a break in the family tradition then, coming up here," I suggest.

He sighs. "I came up here for a woman. Sybil was her name, Sybil Crockett. She worked in the school kitchen. I was with her for three months, then she buggered off with some farmer. Turned out she'd been running us both. He was the winner." He pauses a moment, watching the horses, then continues. "I'd fallen in love with the place by then, so I stayed. I've got two brothers back home, keeping the business up. I'll go back one day, but I'm happy enough for now." A smile brightens his features. "Who knows. Mrs Stanley Tanner may yet turn up."

"How old are you, if you don't mind me asking?" I inquire.

He turns to face me and spreads out his arms. "Guess."

I chance it. "Forty-five?"

"Bugger," he mutters, hands falling limp to his sides. "I'm a few months short of thirty-nine."

I laugh and pat his back. "Don't worry. Mrs Tanner's on the way. You can bet on it."

He elevates a finger. "I'll take that as a promise."

"You have my word," I smile, walking away. "Have a good day, Stanley."

"You too, sir," he says. "Nice talking."

I continue my secret inspection of the village. There are several shops. Hugh must have been concerned that the farm itself wouldn't be able to supply so many new people. I pass by another substantial building, half complete (the village hall?), and see the church going up in the plot opposite. The work has only just begun, the foundations in. It looks as if the building itself will be modest in size, but the grounds in which it sits are extensive. *Burials?* I ponder. Of course – he's even thought of that. I wonder what Cornelius made of it; I should have asked him.

There's more building work opposite the church – cottages probably – and yet more houses rising behind those.

The field at the eastern end of the village extends away into the distance, rises uphill and disappears over the brow. A figure walks towards me carrying a basket. It's a woman, pretty, dressed in cream linen. Sylvie Ardoin. I raise my hand in greeting.

"Bonjour, Madame."

She stops, startled. "You're French?"

"No," I say. "But you are."

"You know me?"

"I know you all."

"I know you all," I realise I've said it out loud.

Dream's overlapping fishing nets melt into a navigable continuity. The gears of time engage, and I allow my consciousness to leak outside my skull.

The bed is warm, the pillow, soft. It's broad daylight. I've slept later than intended.

I turn on my back and listen. Silence at first; then

I hear her. Pad, pad, pad... She's still there. Of course she's still there.

Quiet, tactile, imagining her feet, her legs... ... The ceiling. A few strands of cobweb float in some private draft.

I flare my nostrils, puzzled. Someone's cooking – smells good.

"Well, well, well – sleepyhead," says Alvina Rowley as I enter the kitchen, yawning, greeting her. She continues, "I knew you were thinking of shutting yourself up in the cellar today, so thought you might like a proper breakfast."

I thank her heartily, sit at the table, and wait.

Alvina busies herself at the stove, turns her head and asks, "Is she joining you?"

Alvina's husband, Rodney, saunters into the kitchen, hands in pockets, smiles, and nods at me.

"The nude woman," Alvina clarifies.

I tell her no and explain that I've never seen her – don't know who she is.

"Oh." Alvina seems genuinely disappointed. "That's a pity." She nods at Rodney. "Rodney's very interested in naked women."

"I am," he admits. "Always had a great fondness for them. My father too – also very interested in nude women."

"Oh well," concludes Alvina. "Never mind. It's just you then." She prepares the breakfast items nicely on a large plate: four fried eggs, four devilled kidneys, half a lamb's liver, three square sausages with onion (mmm-mm!), fried potatoes, mushrooms, six slices of bacon, black pudding, white pudding, fruit pudding, haggis, six link sausages, four pieces of fried bread, a two-pound pat of butter and twelve slices of toast – white bread of course, crisp and brown on the outside, with a slender interior of innocent virgin white.

I'm speechless. My wide eyes signal my delight.

"Tea?" she asks, and I nod.

Alvina and Rodney are both plump, happy folk. I happen to know that she is fifty-five years old. I guess he's a little older than she – not quite sixty, fifty-eight perhaps. They'd headed the kitchen staff at the Lookout since the beginning, Alvina doing the cooking, Rodney doing the watching while reading the papers with his feet up at the table. It was a busy life for both of them. I don't know what they did before or where they came from.

"I expect you'd like to know what we did before and where we came from," says Rodney, sitting opposite me, pilfering a piece of my toast and loading it with butter.

I nod, picking bacon out of my teeth.

"We've been in the catering trade all our lives," says Alvina as she begins to wash the pans at the sink. "We're from Wakefield. Both our families, in fact."

I listen carefully, storing the information for later use.

"Kids are still there," says Rodney. "Our three boys: Percy, Peter and Tim. All with families of their own now."

I ask if they ever get to see them.

"Oh yes," says Alvina, splashing away. "Grandkids too; eight o' them now…"

"You alright there, love?" asks Rodney, casting an eye at his wife, busily scrubbing, hands immersed in suds.

"Yes thanks, dear. You know how I love washing up."

It sounds like irony, but I imagine it's true. Washing up in the Lookout kitchen was always done by the assistant staff, so Alvina wouldn't have had much opportunity. This must make a nice change for her.

I'm doing pretty well with my breakfast, and compliment Alvina on it, particularly the lovely, fluffy liver and the exquisitely light black pudding.

"Oh, thank you, dear," she says. "My grandmother Myrtle loved black pudding – never stopped eating it. She used to take it to church for the Eucharist – got the vicar to bless it." Alvina pauses in what she's doing and looks out of the window. I think at first she's looking at Ethel Coombs, but quickly realise she's actually gazing into Bliss's Heavenly Firmament. "Ah," she sighs. "She'll be in Paradise for sure, not the other place."

"Amen," says Rodney. Alvina goes back to the washing up.

I've almost finished eating – on my seventh slice of toast.

"Funny old house you've got here," says Rodney.

"Twists and turns; staircases, landings, ladders, corridors that don't go anywhere, empty rooms, locked doors, pictures hung upside-down, mirrors that reflect different rooms; loads of clocks, all telling different times…"

I'm about to answer him, but Alvina cuts in. "Gene's in the drawing room. We brought him with us – he wants a quick word. Hope you don't mind."

I tell them I'll be pleased to see him, spread the last butter on my final piece of toast, rise, and walk to the drawing room. It takes longer than usual today.

Eugene Fenton, the shyest of the Lookout's four footmen, rises from the sofa and offers me his hand. He's nervous, twitchy. He nods and looks as if he might bow. I welcome him warmly and try to put him at ease. Would he like a drink? I ask.

"No. No, thank you," he replies somewhat breathlessly. I motion him to sit and settle myself into the sofa opposite.

"Thank you for seeing me, sir," he begins.

I ask him not to call me sir, and he apologises. I ask him not to apologise. He says sorry.

Gene is the kind of man you wouldn't look twice at. If you were waiting at tables in a dining room, Gene's is the order you'd forget; Gene is the customer you wouldn't notice. And he's so shy he'd probably rather get up and walk away than draw your attention. He's in his early thirties, average height, averagely good-looking, average brown eyes, averagely brown hair, cut short, clean-shaven. Sadly forgettable.

I ask what I can do for him. He looks at the floor. Clasps his hands in his lap and says, "I'm dull."

That makes two of us, I assure him.

"I'm thirty-two," he says, "and I haven't done anything. I don't want to be forty-two and not have done anything – or fifty-two…"

I inquire what occupies him when he's not being a footman.

He sets his jaw, shakes his head, and says, "Nothing. I mix with the others, of course – but they do things – and I don't."

I ask him about his fling with Clara Sutherland.

"She didn't want me," he replies. "Lasted one night. The only other time I had a flip-flap was five opportunistic minutes in a stagecoach when I was a teenager – and the woman was three times my age – and drunk."

I nod; that *is* bad.

"I'm the one left dangling," he says. "Newt's got Eleanor, Theo's got Sukey, Rye's married to Flossie. Me? Mr Grey, Mr Forgotten, Mr Nobody."

I can see he's properly upset. To be honest, I hadn't given him much thought. Perhaps I could have him drown in the Esk, or be trampled by a bull, or eaten by a shark in Whitby harbour… But these are unkind thoughts, brought on because I know I soon have to descend beneath the house. I try to be kinder and promise him that his day is coming. He'll have a purpose. Trust me, I tell him.

He drops his head, and I'm concerned that he might actually begin to cry. "Thank you," he says.

"Whatever happens, it'll be better than waiting for nothing." We rise in unison, and I extend my hand. "It was worth coming today," he says. "Alvina said you'd listen."

I nod, reaffirm my commitment to him, and see him out into the hall. He stands still and listens to the padding feet high up in the house..., points upward, one finger of each hand, looks at me, and asks quietly, "Is that...?"

I reply in the affirmative, and he listens a moment longer, fascinated. Finally, I open the door for him and watch as he makes his way down the path, lifting his hand in greeting to Theo and Sukey as they intersect on their course. I notice with some surprise that Crispin Stafford and his wife Winnie (née Warwick) are also in orbit around the house, although they're following a clockwise rotation, in opposition to Sukey and Theo. I call out to them and ask how long they've been pursuing their circuit.

"Since before you woke this morning," shouts Crispin, raising his hat. Winnie waves prettily at me. She's dressed in dark blue with a matching bonnet.

I ask what they're doing.

"Waiting," shouts Crispin.

I'm not sure what that means and ask them to explain.

"Waiting for *you*," calls Winnie. "The same as Sukey and Theo. We're *all* waiting for you."

I'm about to answer, but they're moving quite fast and disappear round the side of the house.

Ethel's there, of course, just beyond the apple

tree. She's waiting for me too, almost certainly. She doesn't look up. She's probably seething inside, aware I'm watching her. *Bastard men!*

Splendid smells entice my return to the kitchen. Rodney is leaning back, reading my paper, his feet on my table, smoking his pipe.

"Kippers?" asks Alvina.

I'm delighted. It's been at least a year since I've eaten kippers, probably two years. And I'm very hungry.

"I thought you would," says Alvina. "So I made six for you. Here they are…"

I sit down, and she presents me with the plateful of fish. I tuck in straight away; it's delicious.

"And a bit more toast," she adds, producing a rack of twelve slices and another two pounds of butter. Rodney folds my paper, cranes forward, takes a piece of my toast and proceeds to glorify it from the butter dish.

Alvina lowers herself into a chair close to the table, removes her shoes, wedges her left foot on her right knee, and begins cutting her toenails.

"You don't mind, do you?" she asks.

I assure her I don't mind at all and tell her what lovely feet she has. It's not entirely true, but a bit of flirting goes a long way if one hopes to repeat a particular breakfast experience. Rodney peers at me and knits his eyebrows incredulously at my compliment to his wife.

Alvina (snip!) says, "So, you're going downstairs today." It isn't a question.

I confirm that I am.

"It must be fascinating down there," she says. "You've had such an interesting (snip!) life."

I mumble something.

"Shall I make you some sandwiches?" (Snip!)

I'm grateful for that. She's likely to manufacture enough to keep me going for days.

"Very good," she says. "I'll just finish doing me toes..." *(SNIP!)* A large piece of nail goes pinging through the air, bounces on the tabletop and embeds itself in the butter, where it stands proudly upright like Excalibur waiting to be drawn forth by the King of England. "Oops!" says Alvina, leaning forward and picking it out. "Excuse me." She licks the butter off it and flicks it into the sink. "I should have washed me feet first. The nails are easier to cut if they're a bit damp."

I polish off the kippers, and the toast – and the butter. Alvina busies herself with sandwich-making; Rodney does the crossword. I make a second pot of tea and sit quietly.

"Thirteen down," says Rodney. "Number of Deadly Sins."

I frown and shake my head, then start to enumerate them, counting off on my fingers. But I lose track at four hundred and fifty-three, thinking I may have counted one twice. I throw up my hands in frustration.

Rodney's frowning at me, having been waiting patiently for my answer. "I thought there were seven," he says.

I raise my finger – almost cry *Eureka!* – but he shakes his head. "Can't be right though – there are only five letters. One, two, three, four, five. Yes – can't be seven."

I express my intention to depart to the nether regions.

"Here you go then," says Alvina, handing me a haversack of sandwiches. "This'll keep you going for an hour or two. I'll make some more so you can feed yourself when you come back. We'll let ourselves out."

I rise, heft the sack of food over my shoulder, and thank her once again.

"Enjoy yourself," says Rodney, lifting his eyes briefly from six across.

Hmm.

I turn, leave the kitchen, and walk to the cellar entrance.

The doorknob stares at me. It looks as unenthusiastic as I feel. But I have to pretend I want to go in.

Bugger.

I reach out, twist the handle and open the door, exposing the first few steps down – stone, dark, like a cathedral staircase, worn with the regrets of ages. Sighing, I pass inside and shut myself in.

This is a place in which I used to spend a lot of time, digging around, trying to get to some endpoint. If there ever was a reason for being here, I think I must have found it long ago and not recognised what it was. Never mind. I'd better write a few lines just so you know the place still exists. Then we'll get out.

So I take a deep breath, put my best foot forward, and begin to descend. One step, two, ten, circling anticlockwise – a hundred steps, two hundred. The central pit opens up, and I look down into the deep – down into the deepening, darkening dark. The staircase runs round the edge of the widening shaft. There are many black pits off to the side. I try not to look into those.

I've never been to the bottom of this hole in the ground, so I don't know how deep it goes. I've followed it down for three or four miles, but that's nowhere near the end, I'm sure. At two hundred steps, the shaft is about forty feet wide; a mile down, the width is about three hundred yards. The walls glow a dull green or blue, maybe red – it depends. There are organ pipes down there; that's why I used to come here – to try to find them, to be where no-one ever went. These pipes – I couldn't hear them, but I imagined I could feel them – booming – vibrations so slow, pitches so profound, undiscoverable – deep in the earth, where no light could ever penetrate. Subterranean pipes deeper than any mine, pipes a thousand feet long, murmuring inhuman pitches, a lullaby for an abandoned vision.

What the hell. Seems so long ago I've forgotten what it felt like to care.

At half a mile, I decide I've had enough, so I sit down and unpack my lunch.

I ponder, not for the first time, how precarious is the existence of the house, perched above such an abyss. It's a wonder it doesn't break through the earth's crust under its own weight and tumble into the void, never to be seen again. I expect, one day, it will do precisely that. The crows sitting on the chimney pots will feel it first. They'll rise, screaming, as the house crumbles apart and crashes out of the world – out of existence.

I cast my gaze around me as I munch. If I shout, the echo will continue for ten minutes, so I try not to make a sound.

But I don't know why I'm worried – there's nothing alive down here. Just the wreckage of old dreams, redundant hopes. All meaningless now.

That's it – enough of this gloom. I strap up my haversack and retrace my steps, ascending towards my life. The darkness falls behind me.

Emerging into the hallway, I stand motionless and listen. The house seems empty. There are no padding feet upstairs. Alvina and Rodney are gone. I set down my haversack, shut the cellar door and turn the key in the lock. Then I take the key, open a window, and drop it into a flowerbed. Maybe some scavenging magpie will take it away.

Five large cakes await my attention on the kitchen table, with a note that reads: *Hope you had a good day. I expect you're hungry. Alvina xxx.*

I smile, glad to be back in the daylight.

I changed into my dressing gown and sat at the

window all afternoon, thinking, planning, putting the pieces together, watching the two couples as they followed their tracks – Sukey and Theo; Crispin and Winnie. Polite people. Each time they passed, Theo and Crispin raised their hats and greeted one another. Sukey and Winnie curtsied and giggled. Every time, as if it were the first.

I made myself a pot of tea and wondered if Ethel would like some. I let the kettle whistle for a while, pondering – but decided against asking her. I'd have just got the usual silence. So I took a mug and a plate of Alvina's sandwiches into the drawing room and sat looking out at the grounds, pencil in my hand, pad in my lap, sketching bits of plot, fragments of relationships, people's sadnesses, joys, hopes and memories. All real – all demanding care and thoughtfulness.

The fog formed before the sun set, and it became difficult to see the two couples perambulating in opposing circles. I lost sight of them altogether in less than half an hour, and I wondered if they could see the house. The sky darkened, the luminosity in the fog faded, and the world outside entirely disappeared in swirling clouds. It was as if the house stood in an uninhabited, unformed landscape.

Suspecting I might have a visitor later in the evening, I lit the fires in the drawing room and in my bedroom, poured myself another cup of tea and went back to work for half an hour. The crackling flames brightened the place and chased away some of my melancholy.

If she came, at what time might I expect her knock? I checked my timepieces. The tall clock in the corner of the drawing room said ten past eight; my pocket watch told me it was a quarter to six; the clock on the mantelpiece read twenty past nine. I stepped out of the room and found that the single hand of the hall clock was pointing straight up... ...
... ...

I sense her presence and realise it's *is* – no longer *was.* The air softens, warms; my heart beats quicker.

There's a knock at the door. She knows I never lock it, but for some reason she needs my permission to enter. I step forward. "Who is it?"

"You know," she replies, voice soft.

I lift the latch and pull back the barrier that separates her world from mine. The fog drifts in as she enters the house, her dark blue cape flowing behind.

"It's good to see you," I offer.

"Drink," she responds, removing her cloak and handing it to me. She's dressed expensively, as she often is: a crimson silk gown, a fortune of jewels in her rings, brooches, earrings and necklace – big, lonely eyes.

Persephone Reid.

"Whisky?" I suggest.

"Perfect," she purrs. I know she doesn't want to delay; wants to get on with it. I fetch a fresh bottle and two glasses and rejoin her in the hall. She says nothing, but regards me, waiting to be invited.

I motion aloft. "First floor. Second door on the

left."

She ascends, and I follow.

The fire is burning nicely in the bedroom, but I give it further encouragement with the poker while she removes her jewellery.

"Can you unhook me?" she husks. I unfasten her dress, and she slips her shoulders free.

I pour two glasses of booze, remove my dressing gown (I haven't owned a suit of pyjamas since I was fourteen), kick off my slippers, climb into bed, and watch her undress. She faces away from me, looking out of the window, and turns when she's ready. I open the covers, and she climbs in beside me. I kiss her. I guess it's appropriate, and she doesn't seem to mind.

"Did you watch me?" she asks.

"Yes," I said. "You look good."

"How's my arse?"

Seph has a generous, golden heart; she's also vain as hell. I love both qualities. "You have a very pretty bum," I tell her.

As we embrace, I hear the nude woman pad down the stairs and come to a standstill just outside the door. The floorboards creak beneath her weight. She's listening, waiting...

Seph's noticed her; she frowns – mutters under her breath, "There's someone outside."

"Don't worry," I whisper. "She won't come in."

I used to be a pretty good kisser. I'm still okay, I think. Most of my molars have gone, but the incisors are still there, so I can press – there's a bit of firmness behind the lips – and I've had some reasonable reviews and encouragement. I can bite – some seem to like it.

My cuddles are popular too. It's probably something to do with being a fat man, but my cuddles are sought after. Yes, I score reasonably on the kissing and cuddling fronts.

Sadly, I've never been much of a fadoodler. I've tried – God knows – but it's not really one of my strengths – even less now than in the old days. On Clara Sutherland's scale of ten, I'd score about two – on a good day. So I've been a bit anxious about this moment. Nevertheless, I'm determined to try, and I give it my best effort.

She lies quiet in my arms afterwards, and I feel like a failure. God bless her, she's kind. She doesn't laugh – and assures me it was *nice*. I'm grateful for that.

But I know the fadoodling is not really why she's here. She's here because, after more than thirty years together, Sigbert has left her. And she feels worthless, crushed, rejected, cast aside, pointless, unwanted, lonely, facing old age without a companion. She's here because she wants to talk; she wants a cuddle, affection.

She nestles into my shoulder, and I hear the tears in her voice. "What will I do?"

"You're lovely," I tell her as soothingly as possible. "Beautiful..."

"I'm not beautiful," she says. "Maybe I used to be – not any more."

"You are," I reassure her. "Fifty's my favourite age for a woman…"

"I'm fifty-one," she mutters.

"But you're kind, thoughtful, caring. Meadow loves you."

Seph sniffs. "I know she does. I wasn't much good as a mother. I was bloody awful, in fact. I wanted Sigbert to be pleased – spent my whole life in his shadow."

"Maybe he'll come back. Would you have him back?"

She's quiet for a while. "I don't know. Maybe. We were never married, you know."

"I know that," I reply.

"I was his second. Bet you didn't know that."

I didn't, and express mild surprise.

"Yes. He was married before, properly married, when we met. He left his wife for me." There's another pause. "And now he's left me. Payback."

I squeeze her.

She breathes deeply and goes on. "My father never forgave me."

I turn onto my side so we're face-to-face, and put my other arm round her.

"He hated Sigbert anyway, and decided I was a tart for going with him – brought the family into disrepute. Scandalous. Hmm… He was probably right too. But that's me – loose, easy." There's a long silence; then, urgently: "You awake?"

"Of course I'm awake." I stroke her. She feels safe, I think – at least for now.

"Sorry I'm being a bore," she murmurs.

"You're not being a bore." I cuddle her closer. "You're never a bore."

She moistens her lips and goes on. "My mother died a few weeks after I left. I think she'd been ill, but my father made it sound like she'd died because of what I'd done – out of heartbreak." Her voice falters over the last few words, and I sense how raw her pain still is – will always be. "I didn't see her before she died – I didn't know she was ill – he didn't tell me." She sniffs and sighs. "I went to her funeral… That was a mistake." She pauses again, raises a hand to my cheek, and rubs a finger back and forth close to my eye. "You're listening, aren't you?" she whispers.

"I'm listening," I reply.

The fire flickers, and she settles her head beneath my chin. She has nice hair – grey. I've always loved grey hair. She smells nice. And she's soft – smooth.

"I didn't see my father again. He's dead now. He knew about Meadow but never wanted to see her." She's still weeping, I think – silently. I feel her swallow. "Unforgiving bastard," she whispers.

I ask, "What was your mother's name?"

"Ivy," she replies. "My father was Robert. Robert Sergeant. Good old Bob – Bob Sergeant, pillar of the community. Self-righteous, bigoted arsehole."

I stroke her hair, breathe in its scent.

"My mother's maiden name was Ashford. Do you think I could take her family name? Like going back?"

"I don't see why not," I reply.

"It would be a way of saying sorry – maybe." She swallows again, and I feel her tears on my chest. I almost say *Don't cry*, but realise it might be doing her good. I stroke her instead and kiss her forehead. It's meant to be caring, reassuring.

"That's what I'll do," she says. "Persephone Ashford. That's me from now on. That's my name." She wipes her cheeks, clearing away some of the sadness.

"I like it," I reply. "Has a nice ring. Seph Ashford."

"Can I stay with you?" she asks.

I pause. I think I know what she means and answer yes. She kisses my shoulder and snuggles close.

"Seph," I whisper.

"Mm?" Raising her head an inch.

"I'm glad you're here."

"Thank you," she mutters and settles down.

I watch the firelight play on the ceiling while she goes to sleep. The landing floorboards creak as the nude woman shifts her weight back and forth.

4.

The gathering crowd
Ten women in my bath
Donatien and Justine

I woke late again. Seph wasn't there. The bed was cold, and her clothes and jewellery were gone. An ounce of whisky remained in my glass, but hers was empty. I got up and looked around, hoping she'd left a note, but there was nothing.

I opened the door and listened for the padding footsteps... No sound. Perhaps the nude woman was up there, looking down over some lofty bannister, watching me listening for her, deliberately keeping quiet, making me worry. I half wondered why she'd stood outside the door for so long. Curiosity, jealousy, outrage? A combination of all those?

I couldn't be bothered to cook breakfast, so I sat in the kitchen and began the day with Alvina's sandwiches and cakes.

The daylight was grey, and I wondered what the time was. Ten o'clock? Half past eight? Quarter to eleven? Yes, all those probably, and more. Ethel sat on her bench. Alvina had left a bowl of fruit for me, and I was suddenly overcome with a desire to attack, so I picked up an apple, opened the window and chucked it at the nunlet, hoping to hear it quack. Result! The fruit struck her shoulder. She was startled out of her hate, turned her head and stared at me, dignity punctured, furious.

Men!

I waved and shouted good morning.

"Good morning!" It was Sukey and Theo, smiling at me as they passed, in the mistaken belief that my greeting had been directed at them. I suddenly felt a bit mean, raised my hand and gave them a mock military salute – and as I stood there, holding the posture, my apple came flying back and hit me in the face.

"Bloody get writing!" Ethel screamed.

Crispin and Winnie strolled by on their perpetual arc, Ethel on their left, me framed in the kitchen window on their right. They looked concerned, ready to duck, worried they might be the next target for the incensed nun-in-waiting. Crispin prepared a hand, a shield to fend off airborne fruit, but Ethel had already resumed her seat – and her sulking.

The pair disappeared round the corner of the house, but yet another couple followed behind them – Cady Weston and Sarah Alston, attired in their maid's uniforms: black dresses, white aprons and bonnets. There were now three couples perambulating around the building. I emitted my usual muttered exclamation *("What the f...?")*, hastened aloft, peed, washed and dressed. Minutes later I was in the garden, running to catch up with the two newcomers. They'd gone a fair distance, and I was breathless when I reached them.

"You need the pressure put on," Cady said.

I asked what she meant.

"You know," she replied. "You've got a job to do." She was holding hands with Sarah. I liked to see that. They've been together for years. Cady's thirty-one now, Sarah twenty-nine.

I accompanied them in sombre silence for a moment, then asked Cady to tell me the story about shaving Kate.

"That's not for now," Cady replied. "You get writing, and that tale will come out at the right time. Go on." She made a flicking gesture with her fingers, dismissive. "Bugger off and get working."

Sarah peered round Cady at me. "Clear off," she emphasised. "None of us is leaving till you bloody get started properly."

I stopped in my tracks and watched them walk on: Cady and Sarah, Sukey and Theo, Crispin and Winnie. Round and round and round and round. And Ethel under the tree. I wondered what they lived on, what they drank. But at that moment a shaft of heavenly light like the Blessings of the Lord cut through the clouds and illuminated a trestle table covered in barrels and flagons, manned by the six brewers from the Lookout: Dennis McCallum, David Fielding, Donald Fitzroy, Doug Trivet, Dick Brent, and Franklyn (Daniel) Egan. I widened my eyes in disbelief, my mouth following a second later. Another table stood nearby, where Alvina hummed to herself as she made sandwiches. Cakes were attractively arranged at the table's far end, displayed beneath glass covers to keep the flies off. Rodney leaned back in a convenient wooden chair, his feet on the table, reading my paper.

They were all making a concerted effort, and I began to feel pressured. I stomped over to the brewers and asked what was going on.

"We've got to keep the troops fed and watered," Dick Brent replied. "They're here for the long haul. So are we. And there's more coming." He looked off to the side and pointed. "See?"

I followed the direction of his pointed finger and was horrified to observe old Jack Archer, pipe clamped firmly between his teeth, trundling his almost dead wife along the garden path in a three-wheeled bath chair.

"My God!" I cried and trotted towards him. "Jack!"

He grinned at me, his tanned, weathered face crumpling like an old sponge that might have dripped tobacco juice, and raised his hand in greeting.

"Jack, how can you be here?" I quizzed. "Tessa shouldn't be out."

"We had to come, sir," he explained, mumbling around his pipe.

I nodded and muttered, "You're waiting…"

The gentle inclination of his head indicated *yes*.

"For me…" I finished.

A second affirmative dip of the bonce. I stood, fists on hips, and watched as they joined the orbiting traffic. *Shit! Any more, for God's sake?*

I glanced at Ethel's bench and was mortified to

see Tom Thorne, Chad Sandon and Ferret Colborn sitting on the grass behind her, sharing a huge pork pie and downing flagons of ale. Outrage reddened my mind; I marched over and protested.

"What the hell are you three doing here? You're not even part of the Lookout crew anymore! You buggered off at the first sign of trouble."

"We've come for the show," said Ferret.

"Yeah," said Chad. "Bloody get on with it!"

"...On with it," echoed Tom Thorne. He stood, spat a piece of gristle onto the grass, adjusted his testicles and reseated himself.

I turned round to find Ethel offering me a sarcastic, *told-you-so* grin. *Piss off!* teetered on my lips, but I decided not to give it utterance.

The air thickened – warmed – and I realised I was forgetting something. My vision was drawn to the house, and there they were – a line of women waiting at the front door, smiling at me. Ten of them, each carrying a bag: Nellie Brent, Molly Colby, Jewel Springfield, Tillie Haley, Margaret York, Edie Ashton, Kim Kelsey, Maisie Blythe, Opal Clayden, and Annie Alby.

All the frustration dissolved; my heart melted. *Sanity at last. Bath time.*

They stand in my hall, hatted and caped, self-conscious, shy, all in their twenties and thirties except sixty-year-old Maisie Blythe. Maisie is the natural leader – and the only one not giggling with embarrassed anticipation.

I was expecting Mabel Stanton and ask if she's joining us later.

"Mabel's not coming," says Maisie. "She says you've got enough stuff on her already."

I'm disappointed. I could never have enough stuff on Mabel. She's gifted – one of the few who could see the two boys in the tower.

Maisie senses my regret. "Don't worry," she chuckles. "This lot'll give you enough trouble."

They titter ominously, and I suggest we get straight to business, promising them a glass of wine once proceedings are underway. I raise my right hand, indicating the staircase, and they ascend, a gradient of fizzing femininity, to the first-floor landing.

I'm aware that the nude woman is back. She's being very quiet, but I'm attuned to the sounds she makes, the movement of the air she displaces. She's standing motionless about three floors up, looking down and following events closely. If I raise my head I'll see her face, I'll know who she is. But I'm not sure I want that. I *do* want it, of course, but I also *don't* want it. I've lived with the anticipation for sixty years; there might still be another ten or twenty.

My attention returns to the waiting ladies. They're watching me with slightly puzzled expressions, probably wondering what I'm thinking. I open the door to one of the bedrooms and usher them inside so they can prepare for the bath. A string of girly giggling files past me into the chamber. Twenty-six-year-old Edie Ashton (the youngest) pauses, smiles up at me, and asks, "Shall we put on our bathing costumes?" Her smile darkens, her eyes deepen, and she husks, "Or would you prefer us in our pelts?"

All ten are suddenly still; the tittering stops. Twenty eyes on me, primed, ready for my command.

The thought of sharing a bath with ten naked women has a peculiar effect on me, and I feel the presence of Satan over my left shoulder. He's speaking softly, temptingly, and I listen, my nostrils flaring, the corners of my lips lifting:

Do it. Snap your fingers and they'll shed their skins...

But my better self comes charging to the rescue (damn it!). Concern radiates from above – not from the Lord God, but from the nude woman – and I receive it in my heart. It has to be bathing costumes. I can't compromise the special status of the one nude woman. I remember the previous night and acknowledge that two nude women in the house is the absolute maximum permitted. My regret must be showing in my expression because I see it reflected in the faces of my visitors. I smile sadly and say it had better be bathing suits. In any case, there's probably enough flesh in the accompanying volume, where there's no anxious nude woman to keep watch. They begin to get ready, and I retire to prepare the bath.

The bath in my house is circular and very large, a kind of pit sunk into the floor. The subterranean furnaces that heat the water have been burning for decades, so all I have to do is insert the plug, turn on all the taps and chuck in a load of soap flakes. I watch them dissolve in the rising, bubbling froth. The room fills with steam. I change into my own "bathing costume" (a pair of long white cotton leggings with *MONITUM! HAEC BESTIA MORSUS!* stencilled on the front), hop down into the bath, lean back against the side, and wait for the girls.

Here they come, screaming, leaping across the corridor from the bedroom. There's going to be water splashing all over the place...

First in is pretty little brown-haired Edie Ashton, flying through the steam and crashing into the water. The others follow in rapid succession, so fast I can't make out the order of delivery. I was expecting to see those ridiculous women's bathing suits – voluminous, ankle-length, elaborate, ballgown things – but no. Evidently, when these ladies say "bathing costumes", they mean "shifts". It looks like there's going to be a lot of peeping pink after all.

Maisie Blythe lets herself down carefully into the water at my right. She's only a bit smaller than me – a few ounces north of sixteen stone, I should think. Her shift looks a bit like a tent, and I try not to look as the water seeps through the material and renders it transparent.

"Can I sit next to you?" she rumbles.

I readily grant permission. We're both fat and sixty after all, and I imagine she'll protect me from the predatory younger women nearby. I slither my right arm around her shoulders. She presses herself against me and runs her hand down my thigh. I squeeze her right shoulder.

The bath has become a simmering cauldron, filled with excited, noisy women, splashing and teasing each other as if it's summer at Scarborough seaside.

"You've got a nice chest," growls Maisie, sliding her hand across it. I see the tip of her tongue briefly as she moistens her lips. "I like hairy chests."

I'm not entirely sure where this might end up, so ask her about Birdie Wade in the hope of deflecting possible awkwardness or worse.

"Birdie?" she says. "She's fine, I think. Bit under the weather today, what with her cough and everything."

I express relief that she's not dead.

Maisie stops her rubbing and looks at me, puzzled. "Dead?"

I explain that she was definitely dead just the other day, lying on her back in my garden.

"Oh," says Maisie. "I expect she got better then." She frowns, and continues her exploration of my chest, pressing here and there with her fingertips. "She's not been well for years – but I can't recall her actually being dead before."

I reflect on this for a moment and believe I understand. Birdie's death in the garden was a message from volume two (at least, I guess that's what it was). Sometimes I get these flashes of insight.

Maisie's moved on from my chest. I think I'd better stop describing this – it's likely to get embarrassing. Suffice it to say that my continued conversation with her is not always easy or entirely coherent.

"Birdie's even older than me, you know," says Maisie. "She's sixty-three. Probably the oldest of the domestics." She pauses in her manual exertions, deep in thought, and I take the opportunity for a few relieved breaths. Maisie's thinking out loud. "I wonder if she's actually the oldest person at the Lookout... Hmm... There's Milton York and Janet Illif, of course. They must be about the same age as me and Birdie..." But she's wrong, and I hear the realisation in her voice as she goes on. "Oh, no, I'm forgetting all sorts of people. Chad and Ferret can't be far off sixty. And there's old Rabbit Shipley, of course. He must be over seventy." She nods to herself, relieved to have got it all worked out – and goes back to her task.

I grit my teeth against the renewed onslaught and ask her to pass on my good wishes to Mabel; they're best friends.

"Mabel was thinking about joining us today but reckoned she'd just be wasting the bathwater," Maisie replies. "She says you already know all about her."

It's almost true. There's a bit of Mabel's back story in the other place, but I'd hoped she'd be here today – more so because she might have been able to politely draw Maisie's attention. Never mind – this mauling will give me something to tell my grandkids. Speaking of grandkids, I ask Maisie about hers.

"They're very well, thank you," she replies. "Nice

of you to remember them. The eldest, Ronald, he's seventeen now." She pauses again, and I gasp, momentarily released. "Just think," she says. "I've got a seventeen-year-old grandson."

"What happened to your husband?" I inquire, "… if you don't mind me asking."

"Died," she says simply. "Got ill, took to his bed, and left the world. Just like that. Took less than two days. He was happy, bright as a pin on Wednesday noon, dead by Friday morning. David was his name…"

Her eyes are far away. Her rubbing resumes, though with tenderness. She's thinking of her husband.

"Dead fifteen years now," she says. "He was forty-seven."

I give her another squeeze and pull her a little closer. She lays her head on my shoulder and gives her hand a rest. I sigh in relief.

The others have settled down, and I peer at them through the steam. They're arranged round the circular rim of the bath like knights to my Arthur: Guinevere on my right, Lancelot, Bedivere, Gawain, Galahad, Percival, Tristan and the rest. My knights are almost certainly better-looking, though – and are not wearing armour. I extend my legs and touch toes with them, motioning for Maisie to do the same so we're all connected. Twenty-two feet – soles, heels, a hundred and ten toes – pressed together; each of us quiet, calm, awareness exquisitely focused – the communion of feet more strangely profound than any words.

I don't want to break the stillness. It goes on and on.

One of the taps is dripping – every three or four seconds: drip... drip... drip... drip... drip...

Jewel Springfield sneezes violently; the spell is shattered, and everyone explodes in laughter.

Maisie's massaging my inner thigh. I hold my breath as her fingers probe ever more intimately. Surely, she's not... *Oh! Jesus! She is!* I stifle a yelp, hoping the ladies haven't noticed. Thin, mousy Nellie Brent, thirty-six and Maisie's exact opposite, is sitting to my left. I put my remaining arm around her and invite her to snuggle, partly for solace, partly in the hope it might encourage Maisie to be merciful. Nellie seems pleased. "Ooh!" she smiles. "I haven't had a cuddle since I was sixteen!"

Keeping my voice as steady as possible, I tell her she's most welcome. But within seconds she's groping my left thigh. Oh dear, this could easily get out of control – and I have an announcement to make. I smile apologetically at Nellie, lift her hand from my leg, peel Maisie's digits from my monuments, and call the room to silence. All eyes focus on me expectantly:

I explain why they're here. They were the support staff in the main attraction and didn't get much of an opportunity to reveal their own stories. Now's their chance. I ask them to divulge their secrets, to open the wonders of their lives. I point across the water to little Edie Ashton. She jumps with astonishment and cries, "Me?!" I nod, eyes wide with allurement. Edie flounders, searching for something to say, then raises a finger in discovery. "Me and Margaret..." (she pats the arm of twenty-seven-year-old Margaret York, sitting to her left, blonde hair secured above her head), "...me and Margaret nearly drowned once."

"It's true!" cries Margaret.

(Maisie storms me again, bolder than ever. Fortunately, my tortured cry is mistaken as an expression of empathy for the imperilled swimmers.) Choking, I ask if the near-fatal event occurred at the school.

"It did," says Edie. "It was..." She looks at Margaret and mutters, "How long ago...?"

"1758," says Margaret. "The year after I arrived. You'd only been at the Lookout a few months then, so it must have been in the summer of 1758."

"1758," Edie nods in agreement. "I'd have been eighteen, and Margaret would have been..."

"Nineteen," Margaret finishes.

Edie continues: "It was a nice day – lots of sunshine. And I was a good swimmer – still am..."

"Me too," says Margaret.

"Anyway," Edie goes on, "we were swimming up along the coast. There's this place where a river runs into the sea. Not a big river – but it was running fast that day. P'raps it had been raining – can't remember. Anyway, there we were – not far out – and this big wave comes along. I saw it coming – it was huge! Towering over us. Then it come down, and we got sucked to the bottom of the sea. It was really scary! So I swum up, quick as I could – and there was another wave, just like the first – huge, big as a house – and it crashed down... I only just had time to take a quick breath, then I was on the bottom of the sea again."

Margaret interrupts excitedly. "It was! It was *just* like that! Every wave kept crashing down and driving us deep underwater. We couldn't breathe..."

"I thought we were gonna drown," says Edie, hurrying on. "I remember thinking, I've left me mum and come all the way here, only to die in this lovely place." She covers her mouth with her hand, overwhelmed with the memory. I can't see clearly enough through the steam to tell for sure, but I think her eyes are filling with tears. There's silence, all of us waiting, eager to hear how they escaped. Even Maisie's ardour has paused; she's as captivated as the rest.

Edie isn't able to go on, so Margaret concludes the story. "It was Speck Beckwith saved us," she says. "He was walking his dog along the beach and saw we were in trouble. He just stepped into the waves and pulled us out. Just like that."

A few seconds of stunned astonishment follow. Then Molly Colby says, "You never told us that before."

Margaret shakes her head. "It was a long time ago. Don't think of it much these days."

Annie Alby (at thirty-nine, one of the more senior of the group) pushes her long, greying hair aside and asks, "Why were the waves suddenly so high?"

Margaret shakes her head again. "Don't know. Speck said something about an *underset* – or something like that…"

"Riptide," Edie interjects beneath her friend's account.

Margaret went on without pausing: "…said we wouldn't have been able to get out by ourselves, even though we were close to shore – and the water wasn't as deep as it seemed to be…"

Like the others, I've been swept along with the narrative. I don't know what to say. The two women related the tale with such passion and vividness that I'm stumped for words.

Edie drops a postscript into the silence: "It's true. We'd both have drowned if it hadn't been for Speck."

Several women mutter his name into the hush that follows, and it's like ashes from a funeral pyre sprinkling on the bathwater. I watch my companions in stillness, allowing the moment's solemnity to fully develop, then say quietly, "I'll go get us some wine." I pull myself out of the bath, and my exit in waterlogged underclothes draws hoots of guffaws and a peal of spontaneous applause. "That'll need wringing out!" someone shrieks.

It's a relief to be away from the enchantresses for a few minutes, the atmosphere had become so intense. I glance down at myself and realise how ridiculous is my appearance. Despite Maisie's firm handshake, there's no abiding pain. I pull my garment forward and peer inside, inspecting for signs of damage, bruising or loss. I insert my hand and count: one, two, three; nothing missing, nothing bent, every item accounted for. Thank God! I wonder if my admirer will be upset if I select a different spot for my re-entry into the tub...?

My booze cupboard is well stocked and pretty chilly. Alvina's fruit wine should be more than cool enough to mitigate the steamy tropics of the bathroom, so I slip a few bottles, a corkscrew, and eleven glasses into a sack and return aloft to my eager naiads.

The maidens are parched and voice their thankfulness as I distribute the refreshment. Once the task is complete, I cast my eyes around for a new landing site. Difficult to choose; many of the girls look awfully inviting... But I decide it's got to be Annie Alby, with her lovely silky grey hair. She seems pleased when I drop into the water by her side. Kim Kelsey is on my left. Kim looks modest and tame, thirty-two, slightly built, light brown hair. I think I'm safe.

There's an expectant hush, and I realise with a start that they're waiting for me to say *cheers* or something – to give permission to drink. I do so at once, and we all drain our glasses.

My, we were thirsty!

I encourage them to pass the bottles round, helping themselves, then I request further stories. Any more dramatic tales?

"Well," says Tillie Haley, "I got chased once by Doctor Wayland..."

"Chased?" The word is chucked into the air by several ladies at once.

"Yes," says Tillie. "You remember the summer fair we 'ad five years ago, where Mr Crowan got the acrobats and clowns in? It were a great time – you must recall."

Tillie is in her late twenties and has dark red hair, pale skin and freckles. She's delicate-looking, like a fragile flower. I can imagine Hollis Wayland liking her.

"You mean...?" asks Nellie Brent.

"Late in the afternoon, after we'd 'ad a few drinks and the acrobats 'ad gone, we played Catch-me-if-you-can. Remember?"

A few nods indicate recollection.

"Well," Tillie goes on, "Doctor Wayland chased *me*." She says it slowly, emphasising the word, *me*.

She's got their attention – and mine. We're all silent, waiting for the next bit.

She continues, voice soft and low, almost a whisper. "...into the woods be'ind the maze..."

She's performing this very well, leading the pack by their noses.

"I got away... worse luck."

"Oh, bugger!" cries Molly Colby. "Is that it?" They all jeer, the balloon burst. Jewel Springfield sneezes cacophonously.

Annie Alby, on my immediate left, says, "Opal's got a story." She looks directly at Opal Clayden. "Haven't you, Opal?"

We all gaze expectantly at the accused and await

the plea. Opal reddens and says, "I think I know what you mean, but I can't tell you that. It's not really my story."

Opal Clayden intrigues me. She's a kitchen maid but has the presence and demeanour of a lady. She's of average build, dark-haired with a few strands of grey, looks quite serious – smiles, but doesn't laugh much. I imagine she's thoughtful, kind, intellectual. I happen to know she's thirty-seven.

Annie presses on, a little cruelly, I think. "Whose story is it then? Is it Dick Brent's story?"

Richard Brent is one of the Lookout's brewery staff. I watch this exchange with some unease. Opal looks across the bath at her interrogator and pleads, "Annie – enough."

There's an embarrassed vacuum of voicelessness; I try to puncture it by asking Opal where she's from.

Opal shakes her head. "Nowhere interesting," she says. "I'm from Pickering. My parents worked in the market."

I ask after her parents.

"They're both still alive. I send money home – help to support them. They're getting on now, both in their seventies."

I ask after siblings.

"I had a brother," she says. "But he drowned – more than ten years ago."

I'm sorry to hear that and tell her so. Other voices are similarly raised in sympathy.

Silence returns to the bathroom for a brief moment. Then I express surprise that so many of the women are unmarried.

"We've been working in a manless void," says Molly. "It's not easy to find a husband at the Lookout. Everyone's either married already, too old, or the wrong sex!"

Her comment raises a modest laugh, but I see it's probably true. I ask about romances with people from outside – the farmers or traders who appeared regularly to take orders or deliver goods.

"It does happen," says Kim Kelsey, on my immediate left. "Not very often, though. The buggers are all so bloody ugly!"

"There was Sybil Crockett, though," says Annie, leaning forward and addressing Kim across my chest.

"That was years ago," returns Kim. She furrows her brow, trying to remember. "Wasn't she with Stanley Tanner for a while?"

"She was," says Nellie. "I remember that. She'd have run off with anything though. Dasher she was – wagtail."

But I've got part of that story already, so I stop Nellie in her tracks and ask where she's from.

"Me? No surprises. I'm from up north – Kirkleatham, near Redcar. Me mum and dad both died young, but I worked in the Turner School with me brothers. Cleaners and dogsbodies we were. Me two brothers are still there, but I wanted out. It was too quiet for me. I wanted to marry a pirate."

Her comment draws snorts, cries of "fine chance!" and stuff like that. I ask if she ever found her pirate.

"Plenty of pirates," she replies. "None of them worked at sea, though."

There's more laughter, and Molly Colby passes the bottles round so the glasses can be topped up. Jewel Springfield sneezes.

"Can I smoke my pipe?" asks Molly. I gladly give my permission, and she hops out of the bath and runs through the door. She's a wiry lady: twenty-eight, dark brown hair cut fairly short, sparky, imaginative, quick-thinking. Nice to know she's a smoker.

The rest of the women chat amongst themselves. It looks like I won't get much more material out of them. Molly appears after a couple of minutes, lit-up and trailing a line of pipe smoke. I watch as she lowers herself back into the water. And she watches me watching her. "Fancy a drag?" she asks.

I do, as it happens. She crosses the bath and squeezes in between me and Kim, offering her instrument. I take the pipe and pull on it. It's a good mixture – fruity, with lots of twang. I put my arm round her, and we pass the pipe back and forth.

"What about you, Molly?" I ask. "Where are you from?"

"Wetherby," she replies, and clears her throat.

"Got any stories?"

"Yep. But I'm saving them up for later – you'll have to wait. All you'll get from me today is a share of my baccy."

I nod. Fair enough.

Jewel Springfield sneezes. I call across the pond,

inquiring if she has a cold.

"No," she answers. "This always happens when I share a bath with a man."

The party goes on, but the conversation fizzles. They've got bored with me and aren't going to offer any further morsels. After another twenty minutes they begin to peel off out of the bath. Soon there's just me and Molly. She plants a quick peck on my cheek and lifts herself out of the pit. "See ya," she says, and is gone.

I listen to them drying and changing in the room opposite, chatting animatedly. A few minutes later they march down the stairs and out the front door.

I listen to the house. The tap drips. Drip... drip... drip... drip... There's no other sound. No padding feet. The water's cooling. I imagine vacant shapes where the women's bodies were, holes left behind in the steam. But there's only me now – and ghosts. It's as if they were never here – just me and my imagination; as if I – for some strange reason – had greater substance than they. It's a weird sensation.

Drip... drip... drip... drip...

I lean forward on the narrow wooden chair beneath the stairwell, watch the slow waterdrops from my hair accumulate round my feet, and sense the vast space of the house. I feel the hole of the past beneath me, under the floor. The *now* surrounds me – the today. I hear all the clocks ticking – hundreds of them – softly ticking throughout the house, waiting. I haven't been aware of their ticking before, although I always knew they were there. With their differing opinions. Half past eight; quarter past one; seven minutes past six; ten o'clock; five-and-twenty-to-three...

I listen for the padding footsteps, needing to know they haven't abandoned me, to hear their comfort. But there's nothing: only the patient, ocean-like drumming of the gentle clocks.

I wonder if Seph will come again tonight. I hope she does.

More of them are walking round the house – many more than this morning. Sukey and Theo, Crispin and Winnie, Cady and Sarah, Jack pushing ancient, cobwebbed Tessa in her bath chair – they're all still trundling in their circles. But look at the other couples who arrived while I was entertaining my ladies in the bath: Hollis Wayland and Nana Hall, Tranter and Teresa Tickle, Hilda Dodds and Bonnie Pink, Pammy Heron and Nolly Arkwright, Kipp Nibley and Lettice Shelley, Newt Fallowfield and Eleanor Rodman, Slade Stone and Edwin Elvet, Jude Farlam and Gretchen Ray, John Eldenshaw and Janet Illif (those two always look grim and severe, particularly John, but I know they're warm enough).

Ethel's still there, of course, waiting patiently immobile, like some saint's plaster statue. The three dirty old men watch the house from the edge of the garden: Ferret, Chad and Tom. Alvina, Rodney and the six brewers sit at their trestle tables, keeping vigil, anticipating the first words.

I stick my head closer to the window and peer from side to side, half expecting to see shepherds abiding in the fields. No – but I reckon they're somewhere around.

Alvina's sandwiches are still here. I sigh and stuff my mouth. The bread's getting a bit dry now – I should have covered them. The cakes are good though, particularly the juicy carrot cake with its secret ingredients and lush, deep, sexy icing. The best carrot cake in the world. I indulge myself and suck my fingers one by one…

The evening light glows amber through the whisky and casts the bottle's long shadow across the table. I drink while the sun sinks and listen to the ticking of the house.

There's a second glass waiting.

The lights are off, but I've lit candles and rushlights, hoping to make the place cosy. The fire's alight, crackling, warming. In the bedroom too. I've changed the covers. The bed smells fresh. Cool.

Secret.

Nothing happens.

I'll leave the door open again, as I always do.

There's a knock. I'd given up hope – it's late: eleven o'clock, or ten past nine, or twenty to one.

She knows the door is open.

But it's not Seph.

I'm surprised and squint at my visitors, trying to identify them. The man is in his middle twenties, dressed in a frock coat of fine blue silk, an elaborate white wig, cream stockings, black shoes with silver buckles. He brandishes an ebony cane with a silver handle.

"Come on," he says. "Try harder." He has a French accent.

"Donatien," I say. "What the hell are you doing here?"

"The same as all these people." He gesticulates side to side. I peer beyond him, but the blackness is too impenetrable to see much. There's only starlight, no moon. I regard his young companion: a peasant girl, about fourteen, pretty, dressed in a plain brown frock without ornament. I nod to her. She looks anxious, out of place beside this confident nobleman.

"Where's Kate?" I ask.

"Kate's not here," says Donatien. "You know she's not – you wouldn't expect her to be here." He's amused and wears an irritating grin. "This is Justine," he tells me, indicating the young woman. "Did you know that?"

I shake my head. "No."

He waits. The clocks tick.

"Aren't you going to invite us in?"

I wake from my rudeness, stand aside and motion with my hand. "Of course," I say. "Sorry. I was a million miles away – expecting someone else. Please come in."

He declines. "Thank you, but no. We're not here to have a chat." He looks at Justine and says, "Are we, my dear?"

"Non, Monsieur," she replies, bowing her head.

Donatien looks at me. His fixed grin belongs in an obscene painting. "Obedient child," he says, nodding. "A good girl."

I frown. "Is Kate well? You know how she is?"

"That is not for me to say," Donatien replies. He looks hard at me, and his smile disappears. "Tomorrow is the day."

"It is," I reply.

He nods, and his smile returns. "Then we wish you bonne nuit." He offers me his hand, and I extend mine to take it – but he withdraws his, thumbs his nose at me and waggles his fingers. "À demain!" They turn and disappear into the night.

I take a few steps outside my front door and look around in the darkness. I can't see anyone, but I know the garden is full of people. There's no sound. No owl, no wind, no rustle of animals, no footsteps of unseen folk – only my own breath, suspended above the water of unbeing.

5.

Time to begin

Sunlight wakes me. The air is full of birds: pigeons, crows, gulls...

It must be more than an hour past dawn. I slept with the window open last night, shutters thrown back, curtains drawn aside. It wasn't cold.

Seph didn't come. I didn't really expect her to.

There are voices in the garden – greetings, laughter. The house is surrounded by lives, by stories – even more than last night. I feel the giant fingers of souls fumbling through the window, demanding substance, searching for me as I lay on my back, looking up at the ceiling.

It's today.

For my breakfast, the dry remains of Alvina's sandwiches; then I take a mug of tea and a large piece of carrot cake, and step outside.

It's warm, bright. Someone's singing. I look far over towards the edge of the grounds and smile. It's Mary Acker, head lifted, joyful tears running, singing her heart out. I don't know the ballad but I'm sure it will become familiar in time.

The garden is busy – my garden. Look at them all, these people, these planets, comets. Many raise hands in greeting; a few happy faces call my name.

Some look relieved, others appear apprehensive. I'm glad they're here – all of them.

It's a little surprising to see several folk from the farm; there'd been mostly Lookout people before. Sukey and Theo and the rest, they're all still here. But there's also Tozer and Apple Robinson, both glowing despite the sorrow that's tainted their lives, Grace and Alan Flathers, Amy Swift and Walter Buckley (when *will* they tie the knot?), Doctor Neil Levinson and Nancy Sherborne (if they marry, he'll be her fourth husband), Pond Girl and Rendall Storm. I lock eyes with some as they rotate around the house, and we shine at each other, happy. There's Donatien and Justine. He raises his cane and offers a broad grin; she's more demure, modest, but gives a shy, sideways smile.

Here come the two trios, both circling widdershins, one in the wake of the other: Clara Sutherland (dressed in her usual provocative silks), longsuffering Sylvie Ardoin and Felix Hadleigh. Behind them, William, Sally and Mel Priestly – little Dora, almost two, toddling along in front. Fascinating.

I pick my path through the conflicting orbits and make landfall on the bench near the apple tree, at the opposite end from Ethel Coombs. I set down my tea and take a bite of my carrot cake.

"At bloody last," says Ethel.

I'm surprised to hear her speak, and glance sideways at her, mopping crumbs from my lips. She's looking at me from the shelter of her wimple, nodding.

"Sorry," I say. "Been busy."

"Today then," she says. "Before noon."

"This morning," I confirm through a mouthful of sweetness.

Ethel slides along the bench and sits close by my side. Out of character. She must be dead pleased.

"So, is it a good story? For me?" she asks.

"How can I say?" I reply. "*You* write the stories – all of you. You write your *own* stories. You only *think* it's me."

She's quiet for a moment. "Sounds like an excuse," she says, but I can hear the smile in her voice. I offer her a piece of my cake and am delighted she accepts. I hold it steady while she bites, watching me. It's a strange, intimate sensation.

"Will you stay here?" I ask.

"I like it here," she replies. "I'll stay while it feels right."

I nod, lift my mug of tea and take a swig.

"Shall I make you a cup?" I ask.

She shakes her head. "No. I just want you to begin."

I sit a moment longer, watching all the people. Then I divide the remainder of my cake, leave half with Ethel, and walk back indoors.

I've arranged my desk in the drawing room, in front of the big window. There's ink, a pot of quills and a stack of paper. It's quiet in the house. The padding feet are silent; the clocks hold their breath, ticking stilled. I think of her – Kate – I know where she is, where I'll find her. I listen to my breathing. The air feels clean, cool.

Something's wrong; something's moving, clattering, collapsing, louder, closer... I frown. There's a sound in the fireplace as if someone's cut open a bag of rubble somewhere high up and emptied it down the chimney. Bits of debris fall in the hearth. I'm not sure what to do. Is the house breaking apart? I raise my eyebrows in alarm. Is it the end? Is the building falling through the earth's crust, as I know it must, one day? There's a rumble, a series of thuds. Something clatters out of the chimney, hits the ground, and a cloud of soot explodes into the room. I step back, shielding my eyes.

"Ow! Owowow!!" cries little Fanny Kirkbride, levering herself out of the fireplace and standing up. "That hurt!"

I'm astonished. I hadn't expected to see her again.

"Bloody big place, your 'ouse," she says. "I've been all over it – reet up to 'top." She's black from head to toe, brushing herself down. "D'you know there's a pipe organ in your loft? It's absolutely huge!"

I nod. I always knew it was there – spent my life trying to reach it. But it doesn't matter anymore; I'm on a different path.

"Will you be alright?" I ask.

"Me?" she says. "I'm used to a few knocks. You 'ave to expect it, climbin' chimneys. Could do wi' a wash though."

I give directions to the bathroom, and she's gone,

leaving a trail of black footprints on my nice wooden floor. Water begins to splash upstairs, and there's the sound of Fanny singing happily. I fetch a dustpan and brush from the kitchen and tidy the room. Then I stand in the stairwell and listen. Miss Kirkbride. Should I join her? Offer to wash her hair, scrub her back?

Hmmmm...

It wouldn't be right.

And I have a task.

I listen for the familiar padding steps, straining to catch any hint of them behind the sloshing water. Listen... concentrate... shut my eyes... hold my breath... send my ears flying like birds into the lofty skull of the house... ....

But there's nothing. I don't hear her.

Even so, I know she's there. She'd never leave me. Not till I'm dead or have lost my senses to such a degree that no awareness, no direction, no purpose remains.

She's there. Somewhere.

I return to the drawing room and sit at my desk, look out of the window, follow the people as they pass by, my mind floating, beginning to engage, pulling together forms, rooms, streets...

Fanny comes charging down the stairs, calls "See ya!" and leaves the house. I lean closer to the window, crane my head to the right and watch as she scurries away along the path to the gate. The sunlight is heavy, rich. It's the light of memory, both past and uncreated.

I reseat myself and stare through the glass once more, looking far away, far away... Far away, beyond this existence, this garden. I see the orbits of people further out, over the rim of the world, in the infinite vault. I see... Alice Cromack and her husband George, holding hands, happy. Circled in the telescope of my mind's eye.

The sky is pink all around, beyond the sun, the light filtered through her hair. Kate is the sphere that encloses me – and beyond her, Rose. Consecutive eternities, like ripples in a lake.

My breath comes more easily. I take the paper and dip my quill in the ink.

It's Sunday.

The nude woman enters the room and sits down. I see her reflected dimly in the window, but I don't turn around.

It's Easter 1766.

I write:

The rain sailed in from the southwest, dark clouds saturating the Palace of Versailles and flowing on to drench the city. People caught in the open on the Pont Neuf ran for cover. The deluge darkened the stonework of the Bastille and the abbey of Saint-Antoine-des-Champs, cascading off the buildings and running into the gutters. Church bells rang out the Easter morn, and worshippers hurried beneath their umbrellas, hoping to get to the houses of the Lord before they were soaked to the skin.

A girl lay alone in her bed on the top floor of one of

the tall houses on the Rue Saint-Bernard. She lay on her side, big hazel eyes watching the impact of the water drops on the stone balustrade beyond the open balcony doors. Her hair flowed behind and around her, over the pillows, beneath the sheets, a whirlpool of fire that challenged the rain's ferocity. Kate was seventeen years old, and one day.

Old Emmanuel rang out from Notre-Dame, summoning her to worship, but she didn't respond. She was recalling her birthday just a year ago. Things had been very different then. There'd been no nightmare. She'd been happy...

ABOUT THE AUTHOR

Kevin Corby Bowyer was born in Southend-on-Sea in 1961. He spent most of his life as a professional musician, travelling the world, playing solo concerts, making commercial recordings and trying to teach others how to play. He always thought about his musical performances as acts of storytelling. He is the author of *The House on Boulby Cliff* (2020), *In the Silence of Time* (two volumes, 2021), *Babylon House* (2023), *Cadmun Gale* (2023), and *Splinters of Silence* (2023).

Kevin lives in Scotland with his wife, Sandra.

Printed in Great Britain
by Amazon

37123929R10059